SHARON CREECH

Ruby Holler

SCHOLASTIC INC.
New York Toronto London Auckland Sydney
Mexico City New Delhi Hong Kong Buenos Aires

Ruby
Holler

ISBN 0-439-45808-0

12 11 10 9 8 7 6 5 4 3 2   3 4 5 6 7 8/0

Printed in the U.S.A.   37

First Scholastic printing, January 2003

Typography by Alicia Mikles

For the "J" Team:

Joanna Cotler
Justin Chanda
Jessica Shulsinger

Contents

༰༫

✑ 1 ✑

The Silver Bird

Dallas leaned far out of the window, his eyes fixed on a bird flying lazily in the distance. Sun slanted through the clouds above, as if a spotlight were aimed on the bird.

A silver bird, Dallas thought. *A magical silver bird.*

The bird turned suddenly, veering south over the small town of Boxton, toward the faded yellow building and the window from which Dallas leaned. Dallas stretched his arm out. "Here!" he called. "Over here!"

The bird swooped toward him and then rose up over the building, high, high into the air, over the alley and the train tracks and the dried-up creek. Dallas watched it rise on the air currents over one brown hill and then another, until it disappeared.

He tried to follow it in his mind. He imagined it flying on until it spied a narrow green valley, a scooped-out basin with a creek looping and winding its way through the center. He pictured it swooping down from the sky into this basin in the hills, to this place where cool breezes drifted through the trees, and where the creek was so clear that every stone on its bottom was visible.

Maybe the silver bird had flown home.

"Get out of that window!" a voice shouted from below. "No leaning out of windows!"

Dallas leaned a little farther out and called down to Mr. Trepid. "Did you see that silver bird?"

"Get out of that window, or you're going to join your sister down here pulling weeds," Mr. Trepid threatened.

Dallas spotted his sister, Florida, inching her way along the sidewalk, wrenching clumps of weeds and grass and dirt from the ground.

"Putrid weeds," Florida snarled, heaving a clod of dirt over her shoulder.

Dallas watched as the clod landed on Mr. Trepid's back and as the man scuttled over to Florida and whacked her on the head. Dallas wished the silver bird would return and snare Mr. Trepid and carry him high up over the town and then drop him, *splat,* in the middle.

The Boxton Creek Home

Boxton was a tired town, a neglected place that looked as if it was in danger of collapsing in on itself. A tangle of old homes and shacks clustered around small stores and buildings that had seen better days. One of these buildings was the Boxton Creek Home for Children, a ramshackle house that tilted toward the train tracks and hills beyond. In this building lived the bungling managers, Mr. and Mrs. Trepid; their assistant, Morgan; and thirteen children, ranging in age from six months to thirteen years.

The two oldest children in the Boxton Creek Home were twins, Dallas and Florida.

They were tall for their age, dark-haired and dark-eyed, with sturdy frames and a rough-edged and unkempt look about them. Dallas was the quieter of the two and the one more inclined to daydreaming, while Florida was loud and squirmy, with her mouth full of words bursting out, and her face full of expression, flashing from surprise to disgust in an instant.

The managers of the Home, Mr. and Mrs. Trepid, were middle-aged, cranky and tired, and growing stiff and cold as winter-bound trees. They believed in rules, and their rules were posted on doorways and in hallways and above each child's bed. There were general rules and kitchen rules, bathroom rules and stairway rules, basement rules and outside rules, upstairs rules and downstairs rules, clothing rules, washing rules, cleaning rules, rules upon rules upon rules.

"If we didn't have rules," Mr. Trepid liked to say, "everything would be chaos."

"If we didn't have rules," his wife would say, "these children would eat us alive."

Since Dallas and Florida had lived in the

Boxton Creek Home longer than any of the other children there, they knew all the rules. They also knew the punishments for disobeying the rules, and they knew them well, because they had broken every rule in the Boxton Creek Home. Many times.

"How can we live every day of our lives without running or shouting or throwing or talking or dropping or spilling?" Dallas had once asked Mr. Trepid.

"Thinking Corner. Two hours," was Mr. Trepid's reply.

As he sat in the dark corner of the basement, Dallas imagined a broad field rimmed with trees, and in that imaginary field he ran and shouted and threw sticks and mud, and when he was tired, he lay down in the green grass and felt himself getting smaller and smaller until he was a little baby lying in the grass, and someone with a sweet face leaned down and wrapped him in a white blanket.

When Florida was caught breaking one of the rules, she was more likely to argue and, as a result, to earn extra punishments. She could not

RUBY HOLLER   7

sit still, could not walk when her feet wanted to
run, and so on a fairly regular basis, she'd be
running down the hall and Mrs. Trepid's long
skinny arm would dart out from a doorway,
snare Florida, and lead her to the nearest copy
of The Rules.

"What does that say?" Mrs. Trepid demanded.

Florida squinted at the sign. "'No stupid
running.'"

"It does not say that," Mrs. Trepid said, urg-
ing Florida's face closer to the sign. "Read it
again."

"No stinking stupid running."

"Down to the basement. Two hours in the
Thinking Corner."

"That's stupid."

"Followed by two hours of floor scrubbing."

"Putrid."

"Followed by two hours of weed pulling."

Dallas and Florida had racked up hundreds
of hours in the Thinking Corner, the damp,
dark, cobwebbed corner of the basement. They
had worn the scratchy *I've Been Bad* shirts,

shoveled manure, crawled across acres of fields pulling weeds. They had also peeled potatoes, scrubbed pots and floors, washed windows, and hauled boxes and broken furniture.

"Good hard thinking and good hard work never hurt anybody," Mr. Trepid would say. Mr. Trepid, who was a short, squat man with an awkward walk like a crab scuttling across the ocean floor, did not particularly like thinking or working himself, but he firmly believed that these were good things for children.

The Home was a misfit operation, lost over the years in a larger system. Funds dribbled in, but social workers no longer came to check on the children; health workers and building inspectors no longer came to inspect the building. There was no longer a doctor on staff, or secretarial help. It was run solely by the Trepids, with the help of their overworked assistant, Morgan, who referred to herself as Chief Gopher.

Still, the Boxton Creek Home was as much a home as Dallas and Florida knew. On the front of the building, faded yellow paint curled in strips, like peeling skin. Behind the main building, a string of smaller cubes had been added in a crooked path out the back. Dallas thought it looked like a string of mismatched boxcars laid end to end, and Florida thought it looked like a dragon, with its huge mouth at the front door, waiting to swallow up children who entered it.

When children first came to the Boxton Creek Home, they stayed in one of the bigger rooms in front. But gradually, as the months and years went by, if they'd not been placed elsewhere, they were shunted farther and farther back, to the dark, low-ceilinged, airless rooms at the tail of the house.

"Rotation," Mr. Trepid called it. "Rotation!"

Children came and went. Some were taken in by foster families or adopted. A few ran away but were inevitably returned. One died in his bed, whispering, "Who am I? Who am I?" And although Mr. and Mrs. Trepid had tried their best to move Dallas and Florida out (or rather, as Mrs. Trepid explained it to them, "to find you a lovely home"), the twins were always brought back to the big front door by exasperated adults.

"Trouble twins," these exasperated adults would say. "Nothing but trouble."

In turn, Dallas and Florida had come to think of most adults as *trouble grown-ups*, for that had been their experience, that most grown-ups they'd encountered were short-tempered, impatient, and quick to punish. They had no way of knowing that there were foster parents and adopting parents who were kind and loving and generous and forgiving. In the narrow world of Dallas and Florida, an adult was someone to escape.

Over the years, Dallas and Florida had been squeezed toward the back of the Boxton Creek Home until they'd come to the end of it, where two cubicles huddled side by side. In each was a narrow, lumpy bed, a slim dresser rammed up close to the bed, and a closet. A single bare bulb dangled from each ceiling.

At night, Dallas and Florida listened to the wail of freight trains making their way through Boxton and on to . . . to where? To other places, far and wide. To beautiful places. Peaceful ones. Friendly ones.

Dallas and Florida had a plan. They would not be in the Boxton Creek Home forever. They were going to jump on the night freight train and ride out of town. Soon.

Ruby Holler

Twenty miles from Boxton was Ruby Holler, a lush, green hidden valley with only two cabins nestled in its depths. The cabin at the far end was inhabited by a man who lived on his own and who kept to himself. In the cabin in the middle of the holler lived a sixty-year-old man and his wife.

One warm morning in June, the man and his wife sat on their porch swing.

"Same old view," the man grumbled. "Same old sagging porch. Same old creaky swing."

"You're pretty grouchy this morning," said his wife.

"I'm tired of hauling water and chopping wood."

"Do you think people are right, then?" his wife asked. "Should we move? Get a condo somewhere? Have electricity and heat and a washing machine and one of those air conditioner things?"

Her husband nodded. "And a television, maybe. And a garage with one of those automatic doors."

"That sure would be different," his wife said.

"It sure would," the man agreed.

A small gray bird swooped down from the sky and landed on the porch railing. It cocked its head at the couple, as if it were listening to them.

∞ 4 ∞

Mush

Dallas and Florida sat at their usual places in the far corner of the narrow dining room in the Boxton Creek Home. They were not allowed to sit on the long benches with the other children, because the Trepids didn't want the other children to learn any bad habits from Florida and Dallas. The Trepids would have preferred Dallas and Florida to be meek and cowed, like the others.

Florida poked at the mush on her plate. "Do you think there's any real food in this glop?"

"Might be," Dallas said. "I think I spy a piece of meat stuff." He tentatively stabbed the chunk of meat, imagining that it was steak, the juiciest, best steak in the world.

"Well, I think it's chopped-up cardboard," Florida said, "and ground tree bark with a dash of hog's blood thrown in for color."

She caught the eye of the new girl on the end of the long bench and waved at her.

"Uh-oh," Dallas said, as he spotted Mr. Trepid slipping up behind Florida.

"Ow," Florida said. "What're you whacking my head for?"

"Keep your hands to yourself," Mr. Trepid ordered.

Dallas stared at Mr. Trepid's gold tooth. He imagined himself as a dentist, removing that gold tooth, pocketing it, and refitting Mr. Trepid with something else, maybe something red, maybe plastic, shaped like a fang.

"My hands are to myself," Florida told Mr. Trepid. "Look, see how they're attached to my arms. Quit whacking me on the head."

"I will quit whacking you on the head when you put your hands in your lap, where they're supposed to be."

Florida placed her hands in her lap, and

when Mr. Trepid moved away, Dallas said, "How are you going to eat, with your hands in your lap?"

Florida leaned forward and lapped at the mush with her tongue.

Mr. Trepid returned in a flash.

"My hands are in my lap."

"Eat with your fork," Mr. Trepid ordered.

"Well, how am I supposed to do that if my hands are in my lap?" Florida said.

Dallas was eyeing his plate, trying not to move a muscle. If he laughed, Mr. Trepid would smack him.

The new girl was staring at Florida and Mr. Trepid. "Does he do that to everybody?" she whispered to the boy next to her.

The boy looked terrified. With one hand, he covered his mouth, and with the other, he gestured at the rules posted on the wall. The first rule in the dining room was *No Talking*.

At seven thirty, the buzzer sounded. Dallas washed the last pan and tossed it on the shelf. "To the palace," he said.

Florida raced down the hall. "To the grimy dark dungeon of the decrepit palace."

"Quit that running. Quit that shouting," Mrs. Trepid yelled. "Get in your rooms."

Down the hall they ran, zipping in and out of other children's rooms. The other children laughed at Dallas and Florida, but quickly closed their doors after they'd passed. Laughing at Dallas and Florida was a serious offense, in the eyes of the Trepids.

Once inside their rooms, Dallas and Florida each pried up a loose floorboard and deposited their takings from the kitchen: one nearly whole piece of bread and one raw potato each. It was always good to know that there was something under the boards, something to stave off hunger in the night.

Later that night, Florida tossed and turned. She dreamed about the Hoppers and then woke up, mad at herself for letting the Hoppers into her dreams and now into her waking thoughts.

She and Dallas were five years old when they were sent to the Hoppers. For the first few days, they thought they'd landed in heaven.

They had their own room, and every day the Hoppers gave them a new toy. But then Mrs. Hopper started getting headaches and kept asking them to be quiet and not to touch things. Dallas and Florida tried to be quiet and they tried not to touch things, but sometimes they forgot.

One day, Florida picked up a ten-dollar bill that was lying on the kitchen counter. She was studying the pictures on it when Mr. Hopper snatched it from her and slapped her arm. "Don't you ever steal from me, you hear?"

He looked very mean, way up there glaring down at her. Her insides felt jumbled and queasy.

She started noticing little piles of money everywhere. A pile of bills on the kitchen table. A few more on the bookcase. A jar full of quarters. She wasn't ever going to touch their money, ever.

One day, she came downstairs and saw Dallas sitting on the living room floor, with the jar of quarters in front of him. His hand was dipped way inside and he was swirling the quarters around.

Mr. Hopper bolted into the room and

grabbed the jar, wrenching Dallas's hand out of it. "You little thief," Mr. Hopper said.

Florida seized the jar from Mr. Hopper and smashed it on the floor, sending quarters and shards of glass spattering across the floor like hundreds of silver beetles.

The next day, Dallas and Florida were back at the Boxton Creek Home. Mr. Hopper told the Trepids that he and Mrs. Hopper had made a mistake; they weren't ready for children.

If Florida had been older, she might have felt that Mr. Hopper was right, and that she was lucky to be away from the Hoppers. But she wasn't older. She was five, and what she felt was that she and Dallas had been very bad and they would never be in a real family.

Now in her room at the Boxton Creek Home, Florida wondered why she had dreamed about the Hoppers. They were neither the first nor the last family that Dallas and Florida had been sent to, and they were certainly not the worst. As she drifted back to sleep, though, she was swallowed by another nightmare about the Hoppers.

Next door, Dallas heard Florida whimpering. He crept to his closet and lifted the cardboard flap covering a hole in the wall. "Florida? What's the matter?"

Florida sat up and looked around. She slipped out of bed, tiptoed into her closet, and knelt beside the hole. "I was having a maggoty nightmare about those Hopper people," she said.

"Don't think about them," Dallas said. "Erase them. Someday we'll get on that freight train and ride out of town and we'll be on our own, and we won't have to put up with people like that. Someday we'll live in a beautiful place, and . . ."

On he went like that, until Florida calmed down and curled up on the floor of her closet and fell asleep.

Thinking Corners

Dallas had been showing one of the younger boys how to throw a tennis ball over the roof of the Boxton Creek Home. "You pull your arm back like this, see? And you have to aim high, and at the last minute snap your wrist like this, see?" The ball sailed upward, curving toward the roof, but veered suddenly, crashing into a window.

Now Dallas sat on a stool in the basement Thinking Corner. The first few minutes in the corner were the hardest, because he'd see that damp cement wall and the ghostly cobwebs and spiders, and he'd be reminded of a cellar that he and Florida had once been locked in.

He closed his eyes. *Not going there,* he told himself. *Not going into that cellar. Going somewhere else. Going somewhere green and sunny. Going where there are trees and birds.* And soon enough, he was there in his mind, in the place where trails wound through the woods, and where a boy could throw anything he wanted and it wouldn't get him in trouble.

Two hours later, Mr. Trepid opened the basement door and called down to Dallas. "Out of there, boy. Got another reservation for that space."

As Dallas climbed the steps, he saw Florida standing beside Mr. Trepid, trying to wriggle out of his grasp. "I was just running—I didn't mean to stomp on those flowers," she told Mr. Trepid. "And that hole in the wall—I was just trying to get a little air in that putrid room."

"You just go down there and think about it," Mr. Trepid said.

As Florida passed Dallas on the steps, she said, "My turn. Hope you kept the seat warm."

Florida stomped across the basement room and kicked the wall and the stool.

"I heard that," Mr. Trepid called from above. "You've just earned yourself an extra hour down there."

Putrid man, Florida thought. *Putrid basement. Putrid Thinking Corner.*

She sat on the stool, her arms crossed. *He can't make me think if I don't want to.* She tried to make her mind a blank white canvas, but as hard as she tried, she couldn't keep the canvas blank. Splotches found their way on it, splotches which turned into images, which turned into people.

That morning, she had seen a woman pass by the Home. The woman was tall and large-boned, with frizzy, unruly hair. *That's a little bit like my hair,* Florida had thought.

"Hey, Mom!" she had called.

The woman, startled, turned to Florida, who immediately ducked back in the doorway of the Home. Florida peeked around the door, watching the woman hurry away.

Now in the basement Thinking Corner, Florida saw that woman again in her mind, and she thought, *Well, she* could *have been my mother.*

And that reminded her of the man she'd seen with Mr. Trepid the night before, in the alley behind the Home. The man's back was to her, but he stood in a sort of loose-limbed way, his feet splayed out, his arms swinging at his sides. For some reason, his standing like that reminded her of Dallas. She almost called out, *Hey, Dad!* but then the man had turned, and she saw his matted hair, and there was something about him that frightened her. She was glad she hadn't called out to him. *My father wouldn't look like that!* she thought.

Now she opened her eyes and saw a spider scurrying down the wall. She hopped off her seat, picked up the stool, and hurled it against the wall, smashing the spider.

The basement door opened. Mr. Trepid said, "I heard that. Keep that up and you're going to be down there all day."

The Opportunity

Mrs. Trepid had ahold of Florida's arm and was pulling her down the hall.

"I wasn't doing anything, honest," Florida said. "Where are you taking me?"

Mr. Trepid dragged Dallas in through the back door.

"I was just digging up some worms," Dallas protested. "And are you accidentally squeezing my arm?"

Mr. and Mrs. Trepid ushered Florida and Dallas into their office and closed the door.

"Don't sit down. You're a mess," Mrs. Trepid said.

"I wasn't going to sit anywhere anyway," Florida said.

"Take off those *I've Been Bad* shirts, and put on these clean ones," Mr. Trepid ordered.

"What for?" Florida asked. "You said we had to wear these scratchy smelly putrid things for the rest of the week."

"Take them off," Mr. Trepid repeated. "You two are going somewhere."

Florida flashed Dallas a look. They'd heard this before. Too many times.

"No we're not," Florida said. "We're going to be here until we die."

Mrs. Trepid sank into a chair. "I certainly hope not," she said. "I certainly pray that is not the case."

Mr. Trepid said, "We have an opportunity for you, a splendid opportunity." He looked at his wife. "Don't we, Mrs. T.? Don't we have a splendid opportunity for these two young people?"

"We're not going to any more of those foster places," Florida said. "If that's what you've got in mind, you can just forget it."

Dallas touched Florida's elbow. "Well, we

might, if it was the right place, you know, like a mansion or something."

As Mr. Trepid smiled a slow smile, the light sparkled off his gold front tooth. "This is a grand opportunity."

"I suppose you could consider it a temporary—very temporary—foster arrangement," Mrs. Trepid said.

"Not going," Florida said. "That last place you sent us had more fleas than a mangy dog, and a zillion snakes—"

"Not quite a zillion," Dallas said.

"A hundred zillion," Florida said. "And lizards, and that guy—that guy was crazy. That guy was a lunatic."

Mrs. Trepid winced. "Perhaps that last placement was ill advised—"

"But *this* is a traveling opportunity!" Mr. Trepid interrupted. His tongue slithered over his golden tooth.

Florida and Dallas exchanged a glance.

"What sort of traveling are you talking about?" Dallas asked.

Florida whispered to him, "Don't trust 'em.

Don't fall for it. They're probably sending us to Siberia."

Mrs. Trepid opened a folder on her desk. "Let's see," she said, pulling out a pamphlet. "There's a river trip across the state to the Rutabago River—"

Florida leaned toward the desk. "Huh," she said.

Mrs. Trepid pulled another pamphlet from her folder. "And let's see, there's also a little trip to Kangadoon—"

Dallas strained to see the pamphlet. "You mean the Kangadoon way out in the ocean, that Kangadoon?" In his mind, he had already propelled himself there. He was splashing in the ocean; he was running through the hills.

Mr. Trepid handed the Rutabago pamphlet to Florida and the Kangadoon one to Dallas. "We have a very, very nice and respectable couple—"

"Don't trust 'em," Florida whispered. "Remember that last 'very, very nice couple' with the snakes?"

Dallas saw himself climbing a tall, tall tree in Kangadoon and perching on a branch high above the hills. He had a spyglass and was surveying the ocean, on the lookout for pirates.

Mr. Trepid continued: "And this very, very nice and respectable couple are looking for some strapping strong young people—"

"To do what?" Florida said. "Be their slaves? Hose down their hogs? Clean out their snake pits?"

Mr. Trepid folded his hands, as if in prayer. "This very, very nice and respectable couple are looking for two young people to accompany them to the Rutabago River and to Kangadoon, now, during your summer vacation."

Dallas, up in his imaginary tree in Kangadoon, had spotted a ship far out on the ocean. *Pirates!*

"However," Mrs. Trepid said, "they're not going together. They need one person to go to the Rutabago, and one to go to Kangadoon."

"You mean we'd be split up?" Florida said. "You can't do that. We're not splitting up. We're never splitting up."

"It's only for three months," Mrs. Trepid said. To her husband, she added, "Unfortunately."

Dallas blinked himself back to Mr. and Mrs. Trepid's office. "Do we get to meet these pirates first?" he asked.

"What pirates?" Mrs. Trepid said. "What on earth are you talking about?"

"The people," Florida said. "Do we get to meet 'em and see if they're a couple of lunatics or what?"

Mrs. Trepid smiled. "But of course. Mr. T.?" she said.

Mr. Trepid scuttled out of the office and returned minutes later with a white-haired couple.

"Allow me to introduce Mr. Tiller Morey and his wife, Sairy," he said.

Dallas stared at the man, whose left eye looked a bit droopy. Maybe he'd worn a patch there.

Florida looked at Dallas. "A couple of lunatics," she whispered. "A couple of *old* lunatics."

7

Doubts

Dallas and Florida crawled into their closets and lifted the cardboard covering the hole in the wall.

"What did you think of those lunatics?" Florida whispered.

"They seemed okay," Dallas said. "Better than the usual sort. They smiled a lot."

"Yeah, well those Hoppers and Cranbeps and Burgertons and those creepy Dreep people all smiled, too, until they got a dose of us."

Dallas was thinking about the trip to Kangadoon. He saw himself on the island in the ocean, making a campfire. The waves were lapping in the distance.

"What if these old lunatics are like that last pair?" Florida said. "That slimeball slave driver and his twitchy wife—"

"Maybe these two are different," Dallas said.

"Doubt it. Maybe we should just get on that night train like we planned."

"What about money?" Dallas said. "We need a little money."

"We're never getting any money," Florida said. "If we wait until money falls into our laps, we're going to be here forever."

"You look at your pamphlet?" Dallas asked. "How does that Rutabago River look?"

"Like paradise," she said. "It's probably fake. What's that Kangadoon look like?"

"Double paradise."

"What's the catch?" Florida said. "What do you think is the real story behind these old people saying they're going to take us on these trips?"

"They're not *that* old, and maybe there isn't any catch," Dallas said.

"And maybe there is," Florida said. "I hate it here, but I hate it worse going to these crazy people's houses and getting yelled at and scolded and told that we are loud and messy and stupid—"

"I know it," Dallas said. "But maybe—"

"Yeah, yeah, yeah, you always say 'but maybe,' and it's never any better, and usually it's worse, and I'm sick of it. I vote for the freight train."

"Let's just look at those pamphlets one more time and think about it tonight," Dallas said. "Okay?"

Later, as Florida lay in bed listening to the wail of the freight train passing through Boxton, she thought about the old lunatics and about going down a river in a boat. She wanted to be in that boat on that river, but she wanted to be there with Dallas, not with the old man. She hated the thought of being separated from Dallas. She felt that the only reason they'd survived this long without turning into cowardly wimps or juvenile delinquents was because they'd had each other.

In the room next door, Dallas counted the wails of the train. He saw himself in Kangadoon, wading barefoot along the shore. The sky was blue, the water was blue, the sun beamed down. *Footprints on the sand!* He whirled around, drew his sword.

8

Hansel and Gretel

Dallas and Florida were squashed in between Tiller and Sairy Morey on the front seat of their old truck, bouncing along on the road out of town.

"Where exactly are you taking us?" Florida asked.

"Ruby Holler," Tiller said. He turned to her when he answered, and she saw that he had a pleasant, tanned face, and deep blue eyes. His hair was very white and short, sticking up in places at the back of his head. Up close like this, he didn't look as old as Florida had first thought, but she wasn't going to trust his pleasant face.

"And where exactly is Ruby Holler?" Florida said.

Sairy answered, tapping Florida's arm as she did so. "Down the road a piece, and then down another road back into the hills." Sairy's hand, Florida noticed, was a little wrinkly, but the skin was soft. Florida wasn't going to be fooled by soft-looking skin.

Florida whispered to Dallas, "Those creepy Dreeps lived up in the hills. Hope it's not the same hills."

Dallas cringed, then closed his eyes and tried to picture other hills, rolling ones, green ones.

"How come you're not going with each other on your trips?'" Florida asked Sairy.

But it was Tiller who answered. "Now there's a good question," he said, glancing at Sairy.

He sounded a little grumpy, Florida thought. He was probably going to be the first one to yell at them.

Sairy chattered all the way to Ruby Holler. "Look at that there road rabbit," she said, and, "Over there's where we found a stray lamb," and on like that she went, while Tiller kept his mouth shut and his eyes fixed on the road ahead.

Definitely something bugging him, Florida thought.

As they pulled onto a narrow dirt road, Sairy said, "You are now entering Ruby Holler, the one and only Ruby Holler! Your lives are never going to be the same—"

"You don't have to exaggerate," Tiller said.

Florida and Dallas stared out the window at the winding road ahead and at the tall leafy trees flanking the road and at the stretches of wild grass with blue and red and yellow flowers blooming in thick clumps.

"See over there?" Sairy said. "Bear bush. And over there, tickle-violets."

When they got out of the truck, Florida pulled Dallas aside. "I think these two are a little bit off their rockers," she said.

"Look at this place!" Dallas said. "You ever seen anything so amazing? All these trees? All these hills? Is that a creek over there?"

"Dallas, don't you go falling for sweet talk and trees and creeks. We've got to be ready to flee for the hills and catch that train, you hear?"

"I hope you don't mind the sleeping arrangements," Sairy said, as they stepped onto the front porch.

"Where are you putting us?" Florida asked. "In the hog pen?"

"The hog pen?" Tiller said. "I'm afraid we don't have a cockamamie hog pen. I suppose we could build you one though, if you wanted."

"You got a snake pit?"

"A snake pit?" Tiller said. "You hankering after a slimy snake pit?"

"No," Florida said.

"Don't mind that sagging porch," Sairy said, leading the way inside. "And our place is kind of small, I know." She paused to smooth a quilt covering a chair. "You'll be upstairs."

"In the attic?" Florida said. "You got a dusty cobwebby attic up there?"

Sairy motioned to the wooden ladder. "It's a loft. See? Up there—it's kind of open to everything down below. I hope you don't mind. All our kids slept up there together. I'm sorry we don't have separate rooms for you."

Florida and Dallas scrambled up the ladder into the light, airy loft. Windows overlooked the trees outside and the deep blue mountains beyond. There were four beds in the room, each covered with a brightly colored quilt:

hundreds of patches of red and orange and yellow and brilliant green stitched together.

Dallas gazed out at the trees. *It's like a treehouse up here. A treehouse with beds.*

"Up here? Is this where you mean?" Florida called down to Sairy. "In this big huge place? Or is there a cupboard? You going to put us in a cupboard?"

"I thought you might sleep in those beds. Well, not all of them. Two of them. I hope that's okay," Sairy said. "I hope you'll be comfortable up there."

Dallas sank onto one soft bed. "Florida, this is like floating on a cloud. Try one."

Florida stretched out on another bed. "Probably has bugs in it," she said, jumping up again. "What's the catch? Are they going to fatten us up like Hansel and Gretel and stick us in the oven?"

"Dallas, Florida, could you please come down here?"

"See?" Florida said. "I bet they're going to put us to work now. We're probably going to have to dig a well or something."

Downstairs, Sairy and Tiller had laid the table with a yellow tablecloth. Spread across it was a sliced ham, warm applesauce sprinkled with cinnamon, hot corn bread, and green beans. Four places were set.

It's a feast, Dallas thought. *For kings and queens and very important people.*

"You having company? We have to go outside now?" Florida said.

"This is for us," Sairy said. "For the four of us. Two of us and two of you."

Florida turned to Dallas. "See?" she whispered. "Hansel and Gretel. Don't eat too much."

That night, Dallas fell asleep quickly and was dreaming about his favorite place: a sandy patch of earth beneath a leafy tree, with a curtain of branches dipping down all around him. It was not a place he'd ever seen, except in his dreams.

"Dallas," Florida called, waking him. "Don't you get too comfy. Tomorrow is probably when we find out the yuck part of this."

Florida felt crabby and unsettled, as if it were her responsibility to stay on the alert. Dallas was falling under the spell of all those trees and hills, so she was going to have to be extraready. She didn't trust this idyllic-looking place or that old couple either.

"Dallas," she said, waking him again. "Even if this was a paradise—which it is probably not—and even if you wanted to stay here forever, it's not going to happen. Those people are going to get mad at us before you know it, and they'll have us back with the putrid Trepids before you can blink. So I say we just plan on getting that night train as soon as possible, you hear me?"

"Mm-hm," Dallas mumbled, rolling over and returning to his tree shelter dream.

Florida tossed and turned and eventually dreamed about lizards and rats chasing her through the woods. She was running, running toward something in the distance, but she didn't know what it was she was running toward, and she didn't know why she was carrying a scrunched-up cardboard box in her hands. All she knew was that she couldn't drop the box.

9

The God

Tiller was peering into the mirror beside the bed. "I don't look sixty years old, do I?" he said.

"Of course you don't," Sairy said.

He smoothed his hair with his hand. "And I'm still relatively handsome?" he asked.

"Of course you are."

"You know that lady who was down here last month to buy some of our carvings? That New York lady?"

"I remember."

"You know what she said? She said I was a god!"

Sairy patted Vaseline on her hands and blew

out their candle. "And you believed her, you old coot," Sairy whispered.

Tiller glanced toward the window, at the leafy branch tapping against the panes. *We should send those kids back,* he thought. *Sairy should come with me down the river to the Rutabago, and then I should go with her, searching for that stupid bird in Kangadoon. Maybe I'll suggest that to Sairy in the morning. Maybe I will.*

10

The Egg

D allas was in the cabin kitchen peering at framed photographs on the wall. They were like puzzles. Something in each picture matched something else in that picture, and then something in that picture matched something in a whole different picture.

In the first photograph he examined, the men seemed to have identical noses, long and thin, and they all stood with their arms loosely folded and their heads cocked to one side. Then in the picture next to that one, there were two plump women with that same nose, standing that same way.

Sometimes at school, when parents would

meet their children at the end of the day, Dallas was startled to see how much some of the children looked like their parents. He'd look at a boy and his father standing together and think, *So that's what that father looked like when he was little, and that's what the boy will look like when he grows up.*

"How do we know who we are?" he'd asked Florida. "How will we know what we'll be?"

"We're trouble twins now and we'll be trouble twins when we get old," she said.

"But what will we look like? What do you think we'll be doing?"

"We might be big and clumsy and stupid like we are now," she said, "or maybe we'll get some brains and turn into geniuses or something. How the crawly crud should I know?"

Florida felt uneasy when Dallas asked these questions. She felt as if they had no control over what they were or where they were going or what they might become.

"What if our mother was a big ugly mean person?" she said. "Would you want to know that? Would you want to know that you might turn into a big ugly mean person like her?"

"She wasn't big or ugly or mean," Dallas said. "She was wispy, like a princess, and she was extremely smart, and she could do just about any-thing—she could paint and she could sing like nobody you've ever heard in your life and—"

"Yeah, yeah, yeah," Florida said. "As if you knew."

The screen door banged behind Florida as she entered the cabin. "Dallas, look here, look what I found." In her hand was an egg, pale blue with tiny black-and-white speckles. "Little bird egg, don't you think?" she said.

Dallas tapped at it. "Hold it up to the light. See if you can see anything in there."

Florida held it in front of the window. "Can't see anything except a sort of dark blobby thing. Let's keep it, Dallas. Let's hatch it." She raced up to the loft and put it gently under her pillow. Then she lifted the pillow and shook the egg. *If I could just peek inside,* she thought. She scraped one end with her fingernail. Then she cradled the egg in her hand, warming it. She squeezed it a little.

Crack.

Gooey stuff oozed out of the shell.

"I didn't mean it," she said.

A vague little memory popped into her head. She was little, maybe three? Sitting on someone's kitchen floor. Smashing eggs. One by one: *smash, smash, smash.* All that lovely yellow goo. And there was a jar of peanut butter, too. She could see her chubby little hand spreading it into the cracks of the wooden floor. The peanut butter was smooth and dark and slid into the cracks in the floor.

Slap, slap, slap. Someone slapping her arm. "I didn't mean it," Florida whimpered. Someone screaming at her. *Slap, slap, slap.* Stinging on her arm and face.

Who was that slapping person? Florida wondered. *One of those trouble grown-ups? One of those people who sent me and Dallas back, as if we were clothing that didn't fit?*

In the cabin loft, she stared at the broken egg in her hand, and with one mighty toss, she hurled it against the wall. As the goo oozed slowly downward, she grabbed the pillow from her bed and flung it at the goo, and then she snatched the pillows from the other beds and threw them, one by one, against the wall.

"Putrid egg," she said.

＠ 11 ＠

The Grump

Tiller still thought that Sairy—and not the kid—should come with him on the river trip, but he hadn't been able to find a way to suggest that yet.

Sairy had greeted him in the morning with a kiss on his cheek. "It's so nice having those kids here, don't you think?" She was beaming and bustling around the cabin in a way he hadn't seen in a long time. "So much energy!" she said. "It's contagious."

"Mmph," Tiller grumbled.

"What's eating you?" she said, removing a tray of hot biscuits from the stove.

"Nothing."

"Well, quit being Mr. Grump. See if those kids are up yet. After breakfast, you and Florida can get started fixing up your dream boat for your river trip. She's been feeling a bit grumpy, too, so you two ought to get along swell."

Well, he thought, *maybe the kid* could *help me fix the boat, and then when it's fixed, I'll tell Sairy that she ought to come with me on the river. The kids could go back to Boxton.*

Work

Tiller and Florida were in the barn. "This there's the boat," Tiller said. "It's in kind of sad shape, I admit. My father and I built it over forty years ago. It's mostly a canoe, see? With this specially tailored back end, so's we can hook a motor on it." Tiller removed a tarp from the center of the boat. "Those seats need redoing, and that trim, and there's a couple of leaks, and it needs a fair amount of sanding and varnishing."

"Wait a minute," Florida said. "So I've got to rebuild this boat we're going down the river in?"

"We. *We're* going to fix up this rickety heap. You and me."

"How many hundreds of years is it going to take to fix this thing?" Florida asked. "I never rebuilt a boat before."

"Well, I have. And it won't take years or even months. We're going to do it in two weeks."

"Two weeks? Are you in control of your brains? Oh, I get it. I've got to be out here day and night, hammering and sawing." *So,* she thought, *this is the yuck part. That settles it. We're getting on that train tonight.*

"You only have to work when you want," Tiller said. "You get tired or bored, you stop. How much do you think you should get—per hour?"

"How much what?" Florida asked. "How much water?"

"Earnings. How much money per hour?"

"You mean to tell me you're going to pay me to work? Like in money?"

"Seems only fitting," Tiller said. "How much an hour?"

Florida looked the old man up and down. He was dressed in worn overalls, his boots were scuffed, and the shoelaces broken and knotted.

"Fifty cents?" she said.

"Fifty cents? An hour?"

"Well, shoot, I don't know how much," Florida said. "Ten cents? A nickel?"

Tiller glanced toward Sairy and Dallas on the porch. "Sairy thinks maybe five dollars would be about right," he said.

"An *hour*?" Florida said. "You mean like you'd give me five dollars for every hour I worked? Is that what you're saying?"

"That's what I'm saying."

"Well, squeeze my brains! I'll be out here day and night. I won't even stop to eat. Five dollars an *hour*?" She couldn't wait to tell Dallas. In one afternoon, she'd have enough money for the two of them to hop on that night train and get out of town.

Sairy spread books across the porch table and handed Dallas a pencil and a pad of paper. "Okay, honey," Sairy said. "We're going to start our lists. We're going to need some equipment for our trip to Kangadoon."

"What sort of equipment?" Dallas asked.

"Well, it says here we're going to need backpacks and binoculars—"

"Where do you get stuff like that? The Salvation Army?"

Sairy leaned forward. "I was sort of hankering for new stuff."

"You mean like you go in a store and you buy it—new? Nobody's used it before?"

"That's what I mean. Does that sound too extravagant?"

"You're talking brand-new stuff? For both of us?"

"That's right," Sairy said.

New stuff. Dallas couldn't believe it. He'd never had anything new before. Well, maybe once when he and Florida were little. They'd been sent to the Hoppers, who gave them new toys, but when the twins were sent back to the Home, the Hoppers kept the toys.

He tried to imagine new stuff, shiny and clean, with that new-stuff smell. He could almost see, in his hands, new binoculars, and he could see himself up in a tree, scanning the horizon.

∾ 13 ∾

Gravy

When Tiller had paid Florida twenty dollars for the first afternoon's work, she rushed up to the loft to show Dallas. "We could leave now," she said. "Tonight."

Dallas reached under his mattress and held out another twenty dollars. "Look at this. I got paid, too. It's a bundle—we're rich." He laid out all the money on the bed, smoothing the bills. "You still think they're a couple of lunatics?"

"To give away this kind of money?" she said. "To a couple of kids? Yep, definitely lunatics."

Dallas stared at the money, smoothing it and rearranging it and holding it up to the light. He thought of all the food it might buy: delicious food, sweet food, juicy and fresh food, not the bland, tasteless meals they always had at the Home.

"So are we really leaving tonight?" Florida said. "Are we really catching that night train?"

From down below Sairy called, "Dallas? Florida?"

"Is that chicken I smell?" Dallas asked.

Florida leaned over the railing. "Yep. Dumplings, too."

"I've been thinking," Dallas said. "If we got this much in one day, think how much we'd get in two days. You think we ought to stay one more day?"

Florida watched Sairy down below. "Homemade dumplings, Dallas." Florida slipped her money under the mattress. "I don't see where another day with these here lunatics would hurt too much."

"Yeah," Dallas said. "What's another day going to hurt? We've been waiting on that freight train for thirteen years."

☙❧

After dinner, Tiller was grumpy. "That old well, that old bucket. Wish we had plumbing."

"I like that old well," Dallas said. "Want me to get the water? Show me how."

Outside, Tiller said, "Nothing much to it. Just hook this here rope to the handle, careful-like, and then you lower it down."

Dallas leaned over the well and peered down. "Kinda scary black down there," he said. He looped the rope to the bucket handle and tossed the bucket over the edge.

"Wait—" Tiller said, but it was too late, and the bucket had come loose from the rope, and they heard it splosh in the water below.

"Bucket jumped off the rope," Dallas said. "Got another bucket?"

"On the porch," Tiller said, "but we're going to have to figure out how to get that other bucket out. Don't want it rotting in the water." He was weary. *I'm too old to be teaching kids how to do stuff,* he thought. *I did this all before with my own kids.* "Never mind," he told Dallas. "I'll do it myself."

"Well, what about that wood?" Dallas said.

"You could show me how to chop it. I'd like to use that axe. It'd be just like Paul Bunyan."

Tiller had an image of Dallas wildly swinging the axe, maybe chopping off his foot. "Maybe tomorrow," Tiller said.

"How about that lantern then? Want to show me how to light that thing? It's so cool that you don't have real lights and stuff. It's like pioneers."

Tiller envisioned Dallas knocking over the lantern, setting the whole cabin on fire. "Maybe tomorrow," Tiller said.

"Uh-huh," Dallas mumbled, as if he didn't believe Tiller. Dallas kicked at a rock near his feet, and then he turned and ran toward the creek.

Sairy stepped off the porch. "Tiller, what are you doing? That boy just wants to learn how to do stuff. What's the matter with you lately?"

"I don't know," Tiller said. "I'm feeling crotchety. I want those blasted kids to leave and for us to get back to our life, and why don't you come on the river with me, and then I'll go with you in search of that bird thing in Kangadoon?"

Sairy placed her hand on Tiller's shoulder. "Look, Mr. Crotchety, I don't really have any desire to paddle my arms off, and you don't have any desire whatsoever to go bird searching with me. Admit it. And I know it's not easy for you, suddenly having kids in the house again, but I think we ought to give it a few more days, see how things work out. Now, go inside and eat some cake and quit being so grumbly." She patted his cheek. "And maybe you'd better give some of that cake to Florida, too."

The next morning, in the barn, Tiller said, "Florida, you have a . . . a . . . way with wood."

"A bad way, right?" Florida asked. "I mucked it up, didn't I?"

"No," he said. "I meant that you seem to have a certain idea about how you want to do that trim. It's not how I'd do it, but—"

"I knew it. It's stupid."

"Not stupid, just different." He'd had to restrain himself from redoing the parts she'd already done. She hammered nails so hard that the wood was dented and bashed. The varnish dripped in globs down the side.

"I gopped up that first piece though," Florida said. "Remember?"

"Mm," Tiller said.

"And what about that can of varnish?" she said. "The one I spilled? I don't think any master goes around spilling goop and then stepping in it and then getting it in her hair and then—"

"You know what I did once?" Tiller said. "My daddy told me to paint the barn. Red paint. Very bright red paint. And this old mangy cat kept crawling around my legs, getting in my way, and so I just dabbed a little red paint on its ears, and then it went bonkers and scratched my arm up one side and down the other, and then I dipped that brush back in the paint and flung a whole gob of it at that cat, but the cat got out of the way, and instead I splattered the chicken, and the chicken came after me, pecking and pecking, and I dipped my brush back in and went after the chicken, but the chicken got away and instead I hit the pig and then— well, you get the picture? Pretty soon the whole barnyard was splattered with red paint, and all of the animals were in a frenzy, and my pa came out wanting to know what the devil was going on and—"

"I bet you got a hiding," Florida said. "I bet you got whupped up one side and down the other."

"Well, no," Tiller said. "That wasn't my pa's way."

"It wasn't? You mean he didn't tear you limb from limb and throw you down in the spidery cellar?"

"Nope. What he did was sit there on the fence, with a piece of straw in his mouth, and he said, 'I seen a red cat running through the yard. You see that?'

"'Yessir,' I said.

"'And I seen a red chicken and a red pig— you see that?'

"'Yessir,' I said.

"'Now what are we gonna do about a red cat and a red chicken and a red pig?' my father said.

"And so I had to explain to him how I was going to get rid of that red paint. And then I had to do it. Took me nigh-on two weeks to get all that red paint out of all those animals."

"But you didn't get a whupping?" Florida said.

"Nope." Tiller was surprised that he'd rambled on, telling Florida about the long-forgotten red-paint incident. He felt as if the girl had tricked him somehow. *How'd she do that?*

Florida looked around the barn and out through its wide open doors at the far end, toward an arch of tall leafy trees. "You lived here since you were born?" she asked.

"Nearly," Tiller said. "I was born on a boat."

"On a boat? What happened? Your momma get thrown out of the house and was running away and she stole a boat and—"

"Erm, no. My parents lived on a boat, a little houseboat. Lived there until I was seven. Then we found this place, this land, I mean. We built that cabin and this here barn." *There she goes again,* Tiller thought, *tricking me into talking about old stuff.*

"And your own kids grew up here?" Florida said.

"Yep."

"Then why did they leave?"

Tiller shrugged. "Got married. Got jobs in big cities." He put his hand to his chest, surprised by the sudden sadness he felt. It was as if there were a big empty well inside where his children used to be.

Florida smoothed her hand over the piece of trim she'd been working on. "You didn't whup them, did you?"

"Nope."

"Well, they must be crazy," Florida said, "to leave a place like this, where they could be outside all day, and they could run all they wanted, and they could shout and spit and stuff."

Tiller put down his brush and went to the open barn doors and gazed out across the holler. He tried to picture it as Florida was seeing it, and as his own children had seen it, and as he had seen it as a child.

On the back porch, Sairy read through the list of equipment Dallas had made.

"I believe you've thought of everything, Dallas," she said. "You've got some real good ideas here, things I wouldn't have thought of."

"You're kidding, right?"

In school, Dallas sat in the back. The children in the front had ideas. If Dallas had to do a report, the teacher would say, "Here, John will help you get an idea," or, "That's not what I meant. Let Bonnie show you how to do it," or, "If you can't do the assignment, just sit quietly."

Dallas didn't have parents to come in and look at his work on conference days, or anyone to worry over his report card, so it had never mattered very much to him whether he did the work or not. He daydreamed at school, imagining quiet places in the woods or how cookies were made or how trees grew. He didn't know that these things in his head were all ideas.

But here on the porch in Ruby Holler, Sairy was saying, "No, I'm not kidding. You've got some, erm, interesting ideas. I'm not sure we really need a skateboard, and we might want to add a few things, of course, like maybe sleeping bags and little things like that."

She retrieved a book from a stack by the window. "I want to show you the best thing

now. This is what we're going to find in Kangadoon—this is the red-tailed rocking bird." She
opened the book and held it before him.

"Uh-huh," Dallas said, but a flutter in the
trees distracted him. "Whoa!" he said. "You see
that bright blue bird?"

"Dallas, that's just an old blue jay."

"Well, it's a mighty incredible blue jay."

"It is?" Sairy said, following his gaze.

Dallas made a deep well in his mashed
potatoes and ladled in the smooth caramel-
colored gravy. "You sure make good gravy,
ma'am," he said. "No lumps or anything."

"And it don't taste like possum feet, neither," Florida added.

"Eww—" Tiller said.

"That's a compliment, I think," Sairy said.

In the loft that night, Dallas and Florida
added two sweet rolls and two apples to their
stash beneath a loosened floorboard.

"I don't get hungry in the night here,"
Dallas said. "Do you?"

"No, but just in case—"

Dallas counted his money again. "If we got this much money in a week, think how much we'd get in two weeks—"

"A bundle," Florida said. "We're going to be gazillionaires."

"What do you think gazillionaires do with their money?"

"Heck, I don't know," Florida said. "They probably buy lots and lots and lots of food."

The following night at dinner, as Tiller passed him a bowl of spaghetti, Dallas said, "You two sure go to a lot of trouble cooking."

"Trouble?" Tiller said. "We like to cook."

"'One person's trouble is another person's joy,' that's what Tiller's mom used to say," Sairy added. "Besides, we don't get to cook that much now that our kids are gone."

"How many kids did you have?" Dallas asked.

"Four," Tiller said, lightly tapping his chest as he said each name: "Buddy, Lucy, Charlie, and Rose."

"You miss them?" Florida asked.

"Used to be we missed them every day, every minute," Sairy said. "We couldn't figure out how to fill up our time. Sometimes even now it feels kind of . . . kind of empty here in the holler."

Tiller stared at his wife. *She feels that way, too?* He cleared his throat. "But we got used to it, I guess."

"How'd you get used to it?" Dallas asked.

Tiller swirled his spaghetti. "Well, first off, we made ourselves some getting-over-kids stew, special recipe."

"Yeah, right," Florida said. "There isn't really stew that makes you get over missing your kids."

"We've got some amazing secret recipes," Sairy said. "Beat-the-blues broccoli and anti-cranky crumpets and—"

"Hey, with us here now," Dallas said, "maybe you ought to make yourselves some getting-used-to-kids-again stew."

Tiller reached for a meatball. "What do you think we had last night?" he said.

14

Wood

A row of tiny wooden birds perched on the fireplace mantel, and a fleet of miniature boats rested on top of the bookcase. Florida leaned close to one of the boats. "People can't touch these, right?" she said to Dallas. "I bet if people touched these wee little boats they'd get their hands smacked."

Dallas was nose-to-beak with one of the birds. "People maybe could touch them a little bit," he said.

"They'd probably get shot if they touched these things," Florida said.

The screen door slapped against the frame as Sairy entered from the porch. Both Florida and Dallas jumped back, stuffing their hands in their pockets.

"Were you talking to me?" Sairy said.

"No, I wasn't talking to anybody but the air," Florida said.

"Me neither," Dallas said. "Words were coming out of my mouth, but they weren't aimed at anybody in particular."

"I thought I heard you talking about our birds and our boats," Sairy said.

"Naw," Florida said. "What birds? What boats?"

Sairy slipped over to the bookcase. "These boats." She glided past the mantel. "These birds."

"Well, I'll be! Look at all those little birds and boats, Dallas. You ever notice those before?" Florida said.

"No, I can't say I did," Dallas said.

"Even if I had noticed them, I wouldn't have touched them," Florida said. "People ought to know better than to touch wee little fragile things like these."

"Heck," Sairy said, lifting up one of the

birds, "they're not so fragile. They're made of wood. Here . . ." She handed one of the birds to Dallas and one to Florida.

"Golly, will you look at that?" Dallas said. "It's so smooth. And it's got little feathers carved in and little eyes."

"And mine's got wee feet and a wee pointy beak," Florida said.

Sairy returned to the bookcase. "And these boats, they're pretty sturdy, too," she said, passing one to each of them.

"This one's even got seats and oars," Dallas said. "A little tiny elf person could row this boat on down the river." He tried to maneuver the oars. "*Oops*. Oars came off. *Oops*. Seat got a little smooshed."

As Sairy stared at the broken boat, Dallas took a step backward and raised his arm, as if to shield himself. Sairy moved toward him and gently moved his arm away from his face. "It's *okay*," she said.

Florida inched closer to Dallas. She was balancing a boat on her head and squeezing a bird in her hand. *Snap.* The bird's beak drifted to the floor. "I didn't mean it!" she shouted. "I told you people shouldn't touch them." Florida shoved the bird and the beak and the boat at Sairy. "Go ahead. Punish us. We don't care."

"Punish?" Sairy said. "I'm not a very good punisher." She shrugged and placed the broken bird back on the mantel. "I break things some-times, and when I do, I try and fix them. We'll fix these later." She stood back, regarding the mantel. "We made these," she said. "Tiller made the boats and I made the birds."

"All by yourself? With what?" Dallas asked. "You get a little kit or something in the mail?"

"No, we make the whole thing."

"From what?" Dallas said.

"From wood."

"Where do you get the wood?"

"Look out there," Sairy said, gesturing toward the window and the holler beyond. "There are about a million trees out there in Ruby Holler. That's where we get the wood."

"From regular old trees?" Florida said.

"From regular old trees," Sairy said.

Florida rushed outside and slapped her

hand against the maple tree which stood beside the porch. "Like this one?" she hollered.

Sairy stepped onto the porch, with Dallas behind her. "That's right," she said.

"What do you have to do?" Florida said. "Chop down a tree like this and then hack it up into a zillion itty bits and—"

"No, we don't chop down any trees," Sairy said. "Look in that basket there."

Dallas lifted a cloth off a wide wicker basket. Inside were short pieces of tree limbs.

"We find those just about everywhere. We pick the ones that speak to us," Sairy said.

Florida eyed her. "You think they talk to you? Like a crazy person thinks things talk to them?"

"Not exactly," Sairy said. "You just see a piece and you know it wants you to pick it up and you know there's a bird inside, or maybe a boat."

Dallas examined one of the chunks of wood. "What? Inside this stick thing? There's already a bird or a boat in here?" He knocked one against the porch railing. "How do you get it out?" As he knocked it against the railing a second time, the railing split. *"Oops."*

Tiller ambled around the side of the house. "What's going on?" he said.

Florida and Dallas stepped back against the house.

Sairy studied their faces. "It's *okay*," she said. She turned to Tiller. "Tiller, I think Dallas might want to help you fix this porch. And maybe we ought to do some whittling tonight. Got any extra knives?"

"What are you talking about, knives?" Florida asked. "What are you going to do with knives? You going to stab somebody?"

15

Conversations in the Night

"Florida?" Dallas whispered. "You awake?"

"Awake as an old barn owl," she said.

"You remember when I had to get my picture taken for that passport thing?" Dallas asked.

"Uh-huh. Not the best picture. Your eyes were droopy."

"You know what Sairy said? She said she had to get my birth certificate, too, and I told her I didn't have any birth certificate."

"We weren't born, I guess," Florida said.

"Of course we were *born*. We're here, aren't we? We just don't happen to have any of those birth certificate things in our pockets."

"But you have to have one to get that

passport, right?" Florida said. "Where are you going to get one? Is there a birth certificate shop or something?"

"Sairy said not to worry, that she talked with Mr. Trepid and he said he'd fix everything just fine."

"Mr. Trepid? That pitiful pincher?"

"Hey, listen," Dallas said. "Hear that? It's the train."

Florida heard the faint wail of the freight train as it wound its way through the distant hills, and she pulled the quilt up close to her face. The train sounded so lonely.

In the dark alley behind the Boxton Creek Home, two men met. It was too dark to see either of them clearly, but when one struck a match, the light flashed off his gold tooth.

"Here," he said, passing a wad of money to the other man. "Just keep your lips zipped."

The other man slid two fingers across his mouth. "Zipped," he said. He pocketed the money, turned, and crossed the railroad tracks.

ଚର

In the downstairs bedroom in the cabin in the holler, Tiller climbed into bed beside Sairy and stared at the ceiling above him. "It's weird having those kids up there. Were our kids that blasted clumsy? And did they eat that much?"

"Sure," Sairy said.

"I guess my brain pretty much forgot all that," Tiller said. "Do you think we were good parents?"

Sairy turned to look at him. "Of course we were, once we made our mistakes and got over worrying so much. Sometimes I think we were just getting really good at it when all of a sudden those kids were grown up and gone. Maybe that's why it seems easier to me now, with Florida and Dallas. I figure we know what to expect and we know how to love kids."

Tiller sat up. "But I about died when we were trying to teach Dallas and Florida how to whittle! I thought fingers were going to zing off into the air. Did you see that robin Dallas made—that hacked-up piece of maple he threw down the well? He sure was mad at that hacked-up robin."

"And how about Florida's rowboat?" Sairy said. "Did you see that little thing she carved?"

"Before she buried it? Yes, I saw it. Looked more like a bucket than a rowboat."

"Remember our Charlie?" Sairy said. "When he got so mad at a piece of wood that he set fire to it, and then the porch caught on fire?"

"Oh, yeah, I remember you trying to beat out that fire with my good jacket, and I remember me yelling at Charlie and then feeling so bad afterwards that I made two accept-my-apology pies just for him."

"And out of all our kids," Sairy said, "Charlie turned out to be the one who is a natural carver."

Outside, amid the chirps of crickets, a snowy white owl flew to the maple tree, calling "Hooo—hooo."

Sairy said, "Tiller? You know what Grace told me when Dallas and I were down in Boxton the other day? While Dallas was loading up the truck?"

"What?"

"She said that the Trepids call Dallas and

Florida 'trouble twins.' Grace said maybe we ought to be careful."

"Maybe we've done a stupid, cockamamie thing, taking these kids in," Tiller said. "Maybe we oughta take 'em back."

"Tiller! You can't send them back as if they're a pair of boots that don't fit right. Here's what I think: that Dallas and Florida are no more trouble than most kids, and besides, you might not have noticed it, but I think you're actually beginning to *enjoy* messing around in the holler with them. Don't you make that face at me. You don't have to admit it, but I still *know* it."

Tiller reached over to remove a piece of lint from Sairy's hair. "Well, if we *do* take these kids on these trips—and I'm not saying it's what we ought to do—but *if* we do, at least they won't be together," he said. "How much trouble could one kid be? We each ought to be able to manage one kid."

"But they feel safe together," Sairy said. "Like I feel safe with you."

"Is that a compliment you're giving me?"

"It's just a thing I'm saying, that's all."

❦

"Hear that?" Dallas said. "Sounds like an owl out there." He crept over to the window and peered out.

"How come they call this place Ruby Holler?" Florida asked. "You seen any rubies yet?"

Dallas pressed his nose against the screen. "Sairy told me that in the fall all those maple trees turn scarlet red, and all those red leaves look like a million bazillion rubies dangling on the trees. And she said that now, in the summer, right after a rain, all those leaves look like a bazillion shimmery emeralds, and in the winter, after an ice storm, it looks like a bazillion gazillion sparkly diamonds in the trees."

"Well, why don't they call this Emerald Holler then? Or Diamond Holler? Or Jewel Holler?" Florida asked.

"Heck, I don't know," Dallas said, staring into the blackness. "I feel a mite bad. You know, that Sairy bought me all that stuff and I'm not even going to use it, and she's going to have to go all alone all the way to Kangadoon."

"I know," Florida said. "That ole man

lunatic, he's so proud of our boat, and he'll have to go all by himself all the way down a bunch of winding rivers."

"But we've got our plans, right? We're going to get that night train, right?"

"We didn't ask them to pay us," Florida said. "They *wanted* to pay us. It's not like we're stealing the money, right?"

Later, Florida tossed and turned, slipping in and out of dreams. First she was fleeing rats and lizards, and then she was in a canoe on a narrow river, paddling hard, and then golden light filled up the whole sky and the river, and a golden bird swooped down and sat on her knee and spoke to her. It said, "Have you seen my baby? I'm missing my baby."

Dallas dreamed of the leafy tree with the low-hanging branches. Nearby was a stream so clear he could see every rock and every pebble on its bottom. He could see every stray leaf, every little minnow swimming along. In his dream, Dallas crawled out from under the tree and went to the edge of the stream, where a spectacular silver bird hopped along the bank.

The silver bird stopped in front of Dallas, cocked its head, and said, "There is a place where you can go, where everything is—"

"Is what?" Dallas asked. "Where everything is—what?"

But the bird never finished its sentence.

∞ 16 ∞

The Axe

"Where are those kids?" Tiller asked. "Outside someplace," Sairy said. "Probably climbing trees or exploring the creek." She patted his shoulder. "You missing them?"

"Rubbish," he said. "What's that noise?"

"I don't hear anything."

"That—that hacking, whacking noise—there—hear it? I heard it from down in the cellar. There—hear that?"

"Don't hear a thing," Sairy said. "Guess my ears are going bad, or else you're losing your marbles."

"I'm not losing my marbles."

"Well, then, Mr. Full of Marbles, give me a hand here. Can you reach that top shelf?"

As Tiller reached up, he heard a *thunk, thunk,* followed by a sharp *crack,* followed by a long *whoosh* and *crunch* and a voice shouting, "Timberrr!" He raced for the door, reaching it in time to see his favorite young maple tree crash to the ground. Nearby stood Florida with her hands over her ears, and Dallas, with the axe.

Tiller turned to Sairy, who had followed him to the door. "My favorite maple," he whimpered. "They've chopped down my favorite maple."

"Oh my," Sairy said.

"Hey Tiller! Sairy!" Dallas called. "Lookee here—we chopped down that tree that was in the way—did it all by ourselves—and you didn't even have to waste your time teaching us how to use this thing." Dallas held the axe aloft, triumphantly.

"Restrain me, Sairy," Tiller said, "before I build a snake pit and dump a couple kids in it."

"Come with me," she said, "and keep your mouth closed, if you can manage that, you hear?"

ॐ

"So," Sairy said, after she'd explained that Tiller had planted that tree when their children had left, and he'd worried over it and cared for it and took pleasure from seeing it every day, "you obviously did not know that was a special tree. But we've got lots of old dead trees that could use some chopping. Maybe you could help Tiller do that sometime."

Florida grabbed the axe from Dallas and threw it on the ground. "Maggoty axe. Maggoty stupid axe." She glared at Dallas. "Bet they're not going to like what we did in the barn, either."

Tiller's mouth fell open. "The barn? My *barn*?"

"Might as well get it over with," Florida grumbled at Dallas. "But get ready for the hog pen."

Sairy was patting at both of her cheeks. "The barn? What's this about the barn?"

"Follow us!" Dallas said. "It was supposed to be a surprise—we're not quite done yet, but—"

"Shut *up*," Florida said.

Dallas, oblivious to Florida's warnings, raced up to the barn. "Come on! It's so cool!"

Tiller clutched Sairy's arm as they followed Dallas. Florida trailed them, kicking at rocks and tree trunks as she went. "Oughta just run away right now," Florida mumbled. "Oughta just bury us alive."

Dallas stood in the middle of the barn. "There! Presto! Light!"

Tiller and Sairy gaped at the ragged hole chopped in the side of the barn. Tiller pressed his hand to his chest and sank onto a hay bale. Sairy's hands were clasped tightly together, as if she were praying.

"You chopped a *hole* in the barn?" Sairy said.

"It's a window!" Dallas said. "To give you some light in here."

"A window in my barn?" Tiller said.

"Now, now, Tiller," Sairy said.

Florida was standing at the barn entrance. "Listen, old man," she yelled. "You are always complaining about how blasted dark it is in here and how you can't hardly see to work on that putrid boat. We were trying to do you a favor, but we can see you don't appreciate it. Come on, Dallas, let's get out of here."

"No, wait," Sairy said. "Wait. We're just a little surprised, aren't we, Tiller honey? My goodness, it's been a long time since someone did anything so thoughtful for us, isn't it, Tiller honey?"

Tiller's mouth was squeezed tightly shut, and his nose was wrinkled and his eyes squinty. "Unhh" was the only response that managed to escape his lips.

"Yes indeedy," Sairy said. "Now that I'm standing here, I can see what a brilliant thing that window will be when it's finished. How about that, Tiller? All these years we've lived here and we never had the brains to put a window in this here barn. Isn't that something?"

"Unhh."

ᘖ 17 ᘖ

The Rocker

When Tiller entered the cabin, he saw Florida standing at the door to his and Sairy's bedroom.

"What's that?" Florida asked, pointing to the corner of the bedroom.

Tiller peered into the corner, but couldn't see anything unusual. He scanned the room. "You didn't chop me another window, did you?"

"No."

"Is there a blasted bug in there or something?" he asked.

"No, I mean that chair thing."

"The rocker?" Tiller said.

"That's a rocker?"

Tiller was dumbfounded. "Florida, do you mean to tell me you've never seen a rocker?"

"Well, criminy, I might've seen a picture of one, but I haven't ever seen a real one."

"Now, that's something," Tiller said. "That is a real shame. Here, come sit in it."

"Naw, I'll just break it."

"You won't break it," he said. "Here, look, I can sit in it and it doesn't break." He settled himself in the chair. "This rocker has seen a lot of use. Sairy and I rocked each of our babies in this chair—"

Florida turned, as if to leave the room.

"Wait," Tiller said. "Where are you going? Come and try it."

"You losing your ears? I said I didn't want to."

Tiller sat there, rocking, overcome with memories of babies in his arms, of singing, of patting, of dreaming. It pained him to think that Florida had never seen a rocker.

He found Florida outside, smashing a branch against the side of the well. He stood with his back to her, as if he were speaking to the trees. "Yep," he said, "if someone wanted to sit in that old rocker, that someone could do it anytime she wanted. That someone could rock that chair to pieces. Even if that rocker fell apart, heck, we'd just put it back together." He patted the nearest tree and sauntered off down a trail.

Florida whacked at the well with her branch. "Maggoty old chair," she mumbled.

The next morning, when Sairy and Dallas were outside trying out their compass, Tiller heard a soft *creak-creak* coming from his and Sairy's bedroom. He stood to one side of the doorway, looking in.

Florida was sitting in the rocker, gently rocking, and on her lap were two of the wooden bird carvings from the mantel. Florida was stroking the birds, whispering, "There, there, it's okay."

Tiller stepped away and slipped out onto the porch and stared out through the trees to the creek, and then he looked up the hill toward the barn. He sat on the porch swing, thinking about himself as a child—a skinny, clumsy boy running through the hills and

climbing trees. He remembered his own children climbing those trees and racing to the barn
and all piled together on the porch swing. He
thought about himself in the rocking chair with
his children, and he thought about his mother,
sitting in that same chair. Even when he was
as old as ten or twelve, sometimes his mother
would pull Tiller onto her lap and rock him,
saying, "You're never too old to be rocked."

Tiller wondered what it would be like not
to have trees and creeks and barns, and what it
would be like never to have been rocked.

∾ 18 ∾

The Trepids

In the Boxton Creek Home, Mrs. Trepid sat on the edge of her bed as Mr. Trepid scooted around the room looking for his socks.

"Listen," Mrs. Trepid said. "Hear that?"

Mr. Trepid stopped, alert. "What?"

"Silence," Mrs. Trepid said. "Blissful, peaceful, absolute silence."

Mr. Trepid relaxed. "Ah," he said. "Without those trouble twins, things sure are a lot easier around here." He glanced at his wife to see if she agreed with him.

"Yes," she said, "a lot less trouble." *Less shouting,* she thought, *less yelling, less scolding.* They brought out the worst in her, made her feel so inadequate, but still she felt uneasy now, as she always did when the twins went off to a new home. Sooner or later they'd be back, and Florida would be more surly, and Dallas would be more spacey and clumsy, and all the rules would be broken, and any calm that might have been restored in their absence would be shattered.

Without the twins, there were eleven children in residence at the Boxton Creek Home. On this summer Tuesday morning, ten of them were off at church camp. Remaining was a six-month-old baby, who was now brought to the Trepids' room by their assistant, Morgan, a frail elderly woman.

Morgan tapped at the Trepids' door. "The baby's dressed," Morgan said. "What do you want me to do with her now?"

"I don't know," Mrs. Trepid said, opening the door. "Here, let me see her a minute."

"Oh," Morgan said, reluctantly relinquishing the baby.

The baby stiffened at Mrs. Trepid's touch and then squirmed, as if to release herself. "Stop that," Mrs. Trepid whispered, looking the baby in the eye. "Stop that squirming." The baby instantly stopped moving and stared wide-eyed at the woman holding her. Mrs. Trepid shoved the baby back into Morgan's arms. "Take her for a walk or something."

As Morgan readied the buggy in the front yard, she winked at the baby. "Okey-dokey, baby, Chief Gopher is going to take you for a walky."

Mr. Trepid hurried down the corridors, past all the narrow rooms, to the back door. He slipped outside and scurried down the alley. About fifty yards along was a lean-to shack, which he entered.

Once inside, he flopped into an overstuffed, musty chair and said, "Ah, peace." As he leaned his head back against the chair and closed his eyes, a thought popped into his head: *Life is a fog.* He opened his eyes and glanced around the shack. *Life is a fog? Did I just think that up?* He liked the sound of it—*Life is a fog*—and wondered if maybe he should write it down. Had anyone ever said that before?

He closed his eyes again, hoping that another interesting thought might pop into his head, but instead what drifted into his mind was an image of a boy who'd been at the Home a few years ago.

The boy was skinny and quiet, and one summer's night, Mr. Trepid discovered him lying listless and feverish in his bed. Mr. Trepid summoned his wife. "Do something. He's sick. He's going to die!" but his wife said, "Calm down. It's just a fever. All kids get fevers."

Mr. Trepid had scurried up and down the long halls, uneasy, restless, ending up at the door to Dallas's room at the back of the house. He didn't know what made him open Dallas's door and say, "Hurry! Come with me," and then lead a sleepy Dallas to the sick boy's room. "Watch him," Mr. Trepid begged Dallas.

Dallas sat beside the boy's bed and touched his forehead. "He's very hot," Dallas said. "Burning up to bits."

"I know, I know," Mr. Trepid said. "Should we call the doctor?"

Mrs. Trepid returned to the room. "It's just a fever," she said. "We can't call the doctor every time there's a fever in this place. What's the matter with you all of a sudden?"

As Mr. and Mrs. Trepid stood there watching Dallas place a cool cloth on the boy's forehead, the boy opened his eyes and said, "Who
am I? Who am I?"

"You're Joey," Dallas said.

Joey stared hard at Dallas and then closed
his eyes and stopped breathing.

"He's dead!" Mr. Trepid shouted. "Make
him alive!" Mr. Trepid rushed to Joey and
breathed into his mouth and pounded on his
chest while Mrs. Trepid phoned the doctor.
"Help me," Mr. Trepid urged Dallas. "I don't
know what to do."

Dallas breathed into Joey's mouth, paused,
breathed again. Breathe, pause, breathe. He
could feel Joey getting cooler and cooler.

And then the doctor came and pulled a
sheet over Joey's head and took him away.

The next day, Mr. Trepid went to the ceme-
tery and stood before his own parents' graves.
What . . . ? he asked. *Who . . . ?* But beyond
What? and *Who?* his mind was like a big empty
pot, and he didn't know why he had come to his
parents' graves, or what he wanted to ask them.

Understone Funds

"You smell that?" Dallas asked. He was curled in his bed, yawning.

Florida sniffed. "Pancakes. Maple syrup."

From below came the call: "Dallas, Florida, breakfast is ready."

"Yum," Dallas said, tossing his shoe at Florida. It sailed past her head and cracked the window.

"Oh crud," Florida said. "Just when we'd gone a whole two days without wrecking anything."

"Something break up there?" Sairy called.

Dallas leaned over the railing. "The window sort of got broke," he said. "Little bit of an accident."

Florida joined Dallas at the railing. "*Now* are you feeling like punishing us?" she asked Sairy.

"No," Sairy said. "I'm not. Are *you* feeling like punishing *me*?"

"Why would we do that?" Florida asked.

"Exactly," Sairy said. "Let's make a deal. If you kids won't punish me, I won't punish you. Okay? And Tiller will show you how to fix that window."

Florida elbowed Dallas. "She certainly is a goofy lady," Florida whispered.

At breakfast, Sairy asked, "Anyone seen my blue bowl, the one I usually put fruit in?"

"It's on the porch," Dallas said.

"You mind getting it for me, honey?" Sairy said.

"Well, it's got stuff in it."

"Like what?"

"Just worms and stuff."

"Worms?" Sairy said. "In my blue bowl?"

"With some mud, to keep 'em from drying out," Dallas said. "Want me to get the bowl?"

"Maybe not."

"Is there a rule about the bowl?" Dallas asked.

"A rule?"

"Maybe I broke a rule about the bowl, putting worms in it."

"You didn't break a rule," Sairy said. "Do you *want* a rule about the bowl?"

"No."

"But most people have rules," Florida said.

"I see," Sairy said. "Tiller, do we have any rules here that you know of?"

Tiller scratched his chin. "Let me think a minute. Oh yes, I do believe we have a rule about not letting any donkeys on the roof."

"You goof man," Florida said.

Tiller was making a list of final items needed for the river journey. "One more trip to town ought to do it," he said. "You got enough money, Sairy?"

"Need to collect a little more from the understone funds," she said.

"What's that?" Florida asked. "A bank or something?"

Sairy laughed. "You could say that. It's our

own personal private bank. Two banks, actually.
Tiller has one and I have one, and I'm using his
fund for my trip and he's using my fund for his
trip."

Dallas added more syrup to his pancakes.
"Why don't you use your own funds for your
own trips?"

Tiller said, "This way it's a present. From me
to her and her to me."

"So where are these private banks?" Florida
asked. "I didn't see any banks around here."

"They're not real banks," Sairy said. "Just
holes in the ground. Under stones. Get it?"

"What?" Florida said. "You mean you
buried a bunch of money in the ground and
just put a little old stone on the top of it?"

"Well," Tiller said. "It's a little more sophis-
ticated than that."

"Not much, though," Sairy said. "We've got
these metal boxes, see? And the money goes in
the box in the ground, and the stones that
cover them aren't such little stones. They're
more like . . . like . . . big stones."

"Erm, Sairy . . ." Tiller said. "I don't think
we should . . ."

Florida stopped eating. "Wait. You mean to tell me you've got a bunch of money just sitting out there in the ground? For any old thief to come along and steal it?"

Sairy waved her hand in the air. "Shoot, hardly anybody ever comes through this holler."

"Erm, Sairy—" Tiller said.

But Sairy chattered on. "And how are they going to find our hidden stones out there?" She pushed her hand toward the window overlooking the holler. "You know how many stones are out there? About a million." She smiled, satisfied. "So if you two don't mind tidying up these breakfast things, Tiller and I will go to our private banks and get some money and then we'll all go into town, okay?"

Dallas and Florida stared out the window as Tiller and Sairy set off up the hillside.

"I'm getting an idea," Florida said. "Are you getting an idea?"

Dallas nodded. "I'm getting a tiny little idea about buried treasure. Is that what your idea is about?"

"Yep," she said. "I'm feeling a little itchy to

know where they're going."

"That's in my idea, too," Dallas said.

"And I'm getting another idea that maybe those two shouldn't be out there all by themselves, hiking up those hills, you know what I mean?"

"Heck, they hike up there all the time," Dallas said.

"But," Florida urged, "this time, they probably ought to have somebody knowing where they are, right?"

Through the Holler

Tiller and Sairy had lived so long in Ruby Holler that they knew every twist and turn in it, every path, every foxhole and beehive. They knew where the stream was wide and where it was narrow, where shallow and where deep. They could have made their way through the holler blindfolded.

They were familiar with every species of plant and tree, and although they might not have known the technical names for them, they had their own names for things. There was the picnic tree, with huge overhanging boughs, underneath which they'd often had picnics with their children. Nearby were the tickle-violets which used to make their youngest daughter laugh when she touched them. Near the stream was the bear bush, which had frightened their oldest son once, when he thought it was a bear crouching there.

It was beyond the picnic tree that Sairy and Tiller split up, each heading to the other's understone fund. It amused Sairy, as she made her way through the tickle-violets, that she and Tiller had managed to keep their hiding places secret from each other all these years. Only recently, on Tiller's sixtieth birthday, had she given him a map to her understone fund, so that he could use it for whatever he wanted. And on her sixtieth birthday, Tiller had done the same, giving her a map to his fund, to use for whatever she wanted. She felt privileged now, knowing the way to her husband's understone fund, and she leaped over a log. She felt as if someone had erased thirty years, and there she was with their children again.

As Tiller made his way around the bear bush and across the stream, he, too, was thinking about how he and Sairy had kept the location of their understone funds secret from each other for so long. It was as if they'd had to keep one little secret from each other all those many years, but as to why they'd had to keep a secret, he didn't know.

Then he thought about what Sairy had said about the holler seeming empty after their kids left, and that seemed like another secret they'd kept from each other. He wondered why they hadn't talked about it, why they'd both pretended that it hadn't bothered them that their kids were gone.

Florida and Dallas had only been in the holler a few weeks, and although they had run up and down its hills and shouted across its streams and thrown mud at each other and scrambled over bushes and up trees and spit in a hundred places and dug up worms near the damp creek bank, they did not have very good senses of direction once they were out of sight of the cabin.

"I saw them go up this way," Florida said, "but then they split. Did you see which way they went?"

Dallas was imagining that they were tracking

pirates who would lead them to buried treasure. He narrowed his eyes and surveyed the territory. "Vanished!" he said.

"Shh. I'll go down here—I'm pretty sure the old man went this way. You go up there and see if you can spot the old lady."

"They've got names, you know," Dallas said.

"What are you so grouchy about this morning?"

"Nothing. Just don't like losing their trail, that's all." He crouched low, examined the dirt, and headed up the hill.

Lost and Found

"Dallas, Florida!" Tiller called.

"They knew we'd be right back after we got our understone funds, didn't they?" Sairy said. "Where do you suppose they went?"

Tiller sat down on the porch steps, took out his whittling knife and a piece of wood from his pocket, and shaved slivers from the bark. "Maybe they went chasing after a squirrel or something." He kicked at the shavings near his feet. "I'm not used to waiting around for people. Makes me itchy."

Sairy reached into her own pocket and withdrew her whittling knife and a block of wood. She turned the wood round and round in her hands, closing her eyes and feeling it with the tips of her fingers. As her knife moved nimbly over the wood, shavings drifted down the steps, mixing in with Tiller's wood chips. "Tiller? Know what I was just thinking about? Buddy."

"Buddy?"

"Our son Buddy."

"I know who the ding-dong Buddy is," Tiller said. "I just meant what was it you were thinking about him?"

"Remember when he was, oh, around twelve, and he decided he was an orphan? Remember? That summer, he just up and decided he had accidentally landed in this family and that really he was an orphan."

"And didn't he go live in the barn for a while?" Tiller said.

"Two whole months in the barn."

"Yep, I'm remembering that now. When I asked him what he was going to eat, he said he'd manage on worms and stuff."

"Worms!" Sairy said. "I'm still not entirely

sure what he did eat. I think the other kids snuck him stuff."

"I snuck him some food now and then," Tiller admitted.

"Okay, I admit it, so did I. Left it in a bucket by the barn door."

"How was it he eventually gave up living in the barn?" Tiller asked. "You remember?"

"We made those getting-over-being-an-orphan cookies. Those triple-chocolate things, you know, the ones your mom taught you to make."

"Oh, right. Buddy sure liked chocolate."

"Try calling them again," Sairy said.

"Dallas, Florida!"

From the distance came a muffled call. Tiller and Sairy pocketed their knives and stood.

"I know exactly where that's coming from," Tiller said. "Over by the bear bush."

They found Florida flailing in a patch of briars on the far side of the stream.

"I'm stuck all to bits," Florida grumbled. "Stupid, putrid bushes trapped me."

By the time they untangled her, they heard Dallas calling from the opposite hillside, beyond the tickle-violets and picnic tree.

"Help! Bees! Help!"

"Uh-oh," Sairy said. "Guess we know where he is."

As they all headed back to the cabin, Tiller said, "What were you after?"

"Nothing," Florida said. "We were after nothing whatsoever."

"How come you didn't wait for us?" Sairy said. "We said we'd be right back, didn't we?"

Dallas was still swatting at the air, waving away bees that had long since vanished.

"We were just worried," Florida said. "Weren't we, Dallas? We were just worried maybe you'd get lost or hurt out there."

"Lost?" Tiller said. "Us? Not very likely. We know this place inside and out, backwards and forwards, up and down."

"But it was nice of you to think of us," Sairy said. "We aren't used to anybody worrying about what happens to us old codgers."

❦

Tiller and Sairy sat on the porch swing. In the distance, Dallas and Florida were digging along the creek bank.

"We shouldn't have mentioned our understone funds in front of those kids," Tiller said.

"Why not?"

Tiller rubbed at his jaw. "Just don't think it's a good idea, those kids knowing we've got money buried out there."

"You're not saying they'd steal it, are you?"

"Don't exactly know what I'm saying. Just think it's a little too much temptation for kids who have so little."

Dallas dug in the muddy creek bank. "You almost got us in a lot of trouble, Florida."

"I did not. What're you talking about?"

Dallas pulled a long red worm from the soil. "That idea of yours to follow them and find out where their money was."

"That wasn't my idea. That was your idea," Florida said.

"Was not."

"Was too." Florida tossed a muddy stone at Dallas. "I was just concerned about their safety, that's all."

"Me too," Dallas said, flinging his worm at her.

"Cut that out." Florida cupped the worm and set it back in the mud. "How much money do you think they've got out there?"

"No idea."

"Probably a zillion zillion bazillion dollars." Florida waded out into the water, stepping from stone to stone across the creek. She thought about touching the Hoppers' money and how mad Mr. Hopper had been, and how mad *she* got when Mr. Hopper pulled the jar of quarters away from Dallas and yelled at him. She thought about how she'd grabbed that jar and smashed it and all those quarters and bits of glass went shooting across the floor.

Florida stepped across the stones in the creek and said, "Dallas, money is trouble. I don't want to know where their money is. I never, never, ever want to know where it is."

"Hey!" Dallas said. "I've got an idea. Let's bury *our* money."

"What? Like under stones, you mean?"

"Yeah, it'd be so cool, like buried treasure. Our own buried treasure."

"But we're leaving pretty soon, aren't we?"

"Sure," Dallas said. "But meantime, let's bury the money, okay?"

"Whatever you say, bossy Dallas."

22

A Trip to Boxton

Dallas and Florida had returned to Boxton several times with Tiller and Sairy, and each time the twins had made it clear that they did not want to go near the faded yellow Boxton Creek Home leaning toward the railroad tracks.

"Don't you want to visit your friends there?" Sairy asked.

"The ones we know, they're probably gone already," Florida said.

"Kids go in and out of there that fast?" Tiller asked.

"Like a revolving door," Dallas said.

"And how long have you two been there?"

Sairy asked. "Do you mind if I ask you that?"

"What's to mind?" Florida said. "We've been there longer than anybody. We've been there a zillion years."

"Our revolving door sweeps us right back in there," Dallas said.

"Oh," Sairy said.

"We're trouble," Florida said. "Double trouble."

"You know what our son Buddy used to call himself?" Sairy said. "*Mr. Trouble.* He wasn't any more trouble than any of the other kids, but one summer, he got it in his head that he couldn't do anything right." As they drove out of the holler, Sairy told them the story of how Buddy had decided that he was an orphan and had lived in the barn one summer until Tiller and Sairy made the getting-over-being-an-orphan triple-chocolate cookies.

"Why'd you tell us that story?" Florida said.

"I don't know," Sairy said. "It just popped into my head. You know what? I just realized something. Me and Tiller are orphans, too."

"You're not," Dallas said.

"Technically, yes, we are," Sairy said. "Our parents are no longer living."

"It's not the same thing," Florida said.

Sairy patted Florida's hand. "You're right, Florida. That was a stupid thing for me to say, and I'm sorry my brain popped it out of my mouth."

"Hey," Florida said. "You know those triple-chocolate cookies you made yesterday? Were those by any chance getting-over-being-an-orphan cookies?"

Sairy nudged Tiller. "Tiller? Is that the recipe you used?"

"Can't rightly say for sure," Tiller said. "Enough of this chatter. Here's Boxton. Let's get our plans straight."

Sairy said, "I know you don't want to hear this, but we really should make a stop to see Mr. and Mrs. Trep—"

"Don't say it," Florida said. "Don't you say their names. We're not going. Don't you go, neither."

"That's right," Dallas said. "If we set foot in there, they'll throw us in those cobwebby rooms and lock the doors."

"Oh now," Sairy said, "I do think you might be exaggerating a mite——"

"No way," Florida said. "I'll jump out of this truck right now if you say we have to go there."

"Okay, okay," Sairy said. "You don't have to go. Don't worry. We'll all meet up at Grace's Diner. How's that?"

While the others did their errands, Sairy slipped around the back of the courthouse and down the alley, which was bordered on one side by railroad tracks and on the other side by a sprawling field dotted with junk cars and shacks. She could see the tilting Boxton Creek Home ahead. The alley was littered with crumpled papers and dented hubcaps, with old rubber tires and empty pop cans, and Sairy quickened her pace, feeling uneasy in this unfamiliar place.

Dallas and Florida were standing on the sidewalk outside Grace's Diner when the door opened, and out shuffled Mr. Trepid.

"Well, well, well," he said. "Trouble twins."

Dallas and Florida backed away.

Doughnut crumbs clung to the front of Mr. Trepid's shimmery blue shirt. "Where are those people—that old couple? They're not bringing you back, are they?"

Florida took another two steps backward. "No, they're not bringing us back. They're getting stuff for our trips."

"Oh?" Mr. Trepid glanced across the street at the redbrick bank standing on the corner. "They in there? Getting piles of money?"

"At that stupid bank?" Florida said. "No way. They don't need banks."

"They don't?" Mr. Trepid picked a crumb off his shirt and popped it into his mouth. "It was my distinct understanding that those two had piles of money. *Piles* of it. Collectors pay a lot of money for those little carvings they make."

"Well, they don't need to keep their money in any stupid bank," Florida said. "They've got understone funds."

"Yeah," Dallas said. "They've got their own private banks out in the holler, buried under stones."

"Is that right?" Mr. Trepid said. "How clever."

"And me and Dallas have our own under-stone funds," Florida said.

"How charming," Mr. Trepid said, glancing at his watch. "And when is it you're all heading out on your trips?"

"Right soon," Florida said.

Mr. Trepid looked up at the sky. "Very good indeed. I wish you all well." Then, flicking at the rest of the crumbs on his shirt, he said, "Must be off," and on down the sidewalk he scurried.

"What's he so happy about?" Dallas asked.

"He got rid of us, that's what," Florida said.

Sairy made her way through the littered alley and approached the Boxton Creek Home from the back. As she was rounding the side, she heard Mrs. Trepid's voice.

"Stop that this instant," Mrs. Trepid commanded. "Hush."

Sairy heard a baby cry and saw Mrs. Trepid leaning over a baby carriage, her face bent down close to the crying occupant. "Stop that," Mrs. Trepid repeated.

"Is that a baby you're scolding?" Sairy said.

Mrs. Trepid straightened quickly and turned to Sairy. "This baby is so fussy," she said. "Just like those twins were."

Sairy nodded. "Babies can be that way."

Mrs. Trepid looked annoyed. "You make it sound normal. Doesn't feel normal to me. Drives me crazy!" Mrs. Trepid glanced around the side of the house. "Are you bringing the twins back?"

"No," Sairy said. "Not yet. Your husband asked me to pick up Dallas's passport here."

"Oh," Mrs. Trepid said. "Well, then, go inside. Morgan will find it for you. Mr. T. isn't here." She jiggled the buggy. "Aren't you supposed to leave some money?"

"Am I?" Sairy said.

"Yes, for the passport and all the trouble he went to."

"Was it so very much trouble?"

"Yes," Mrs. Trepid said. "I believe you owe him three hundred dollars."

"Three hundred dollars? Really? My passport was much, much, much less than that."

"The rest is for all the trouble," Mrs. Trepid said, "and for transportation and documents and such."

As Sairy turned to go inside, Mrs. Trepid said, "The twins? How are they?"

"They're fine," Sairy said. "No trouble at all."

23

Ready

Florida ran her hand over the edge of the boat. She couldn't believe that she and Tiller had fixed this boat, and she almost wished there were something else to build. *Maybe this is one thing I'm not too awful at,* she thought. *Maybe my mother or father were builders-of-things.* She glanced around the barn and up at the old stained rafters, feeling a little sad that this was the end of it and the old man didn't even know it.

Inside the cabin, she found Dallas in the loft trying on his new hiking boots.

"Boat's done," Florida said. "Want to see it?"

"It's done? All completely done?"

"Yep. Where's the old lady?"

"Her name is *Sairy*," Dallas said. "Quit calling her 'the old lady.'"

"I'll call her whatever I want to call her," Florida said. "Quit telling me what to do. You're not my boss. Who said you were my boss?"

That afternoon, they retrieved their buried money, and that night in the loft, they stashed some in their shoes, some in their pockets, and some in their backpacks.

"I'm leaving enough money to pay for these backpacks they bought us," Dallas said. "And for this flashlight and these boots. They'll come in handy. And I'll leave some money for these whittling knives, too."

"And I'll leave some for these sleeping bags," Florida said. "We could sure use these sleeping bags. If we leave the money, that's fair, isn't it? It's not like we're taking anything then, right?"

"Right," Dallas said. "Now we'll just wait until they're asleep."

"And then we're out of here," Florida said. "Night train, here we come!"

Dallas and Florida were quiet, facing the windows, waiting for the owl. They were each feeling jittery and mournful, and neither of them could figure out why that was so, since they'd been waiting for this night for a long, long time.

"Tiller?" Sairy said. "You asleep yet?"

"I *was* asleep until you woke me up," Tiller said.

"But you're awake now?"

"Do I have a choice in this matter?"

"Of course you have a choice," Sairy said. "I'm not going to force you to stay awake."

Tiller yawned. "Did you want something?"

"Remember when Dallas and Florida first came here and you asked them how old they were and when their birthday was? You remember that?"

"Yep."

"You remember when their birthday is?"

"The twenty-ninth day of July," Tiller said. "That's why you woke me up?"

Sairy whispered, "You remember Mr.

Trepid said he'd take care of Dallas's passport application and getting his birth certificate and all that?"

"I remember. I haven't completely lost my brains."

Sairy tapped his forehead. "I know that. I was looking at that passport today. The thing is, their birthday isn't the twenty-ninth of July. It's the third of March."

"Kind of a big difference," Tiller said. "March to July—"

"Why do you think they don't know when their real birthday is?" Sairy said.

"Sairy, at this hour of the night, I don't think much of anything. My brains are shut down. The motor's off. The engine's—"

"Okay, okay, okay. I get the picture," Sairy said, blowing out their candle.

Tiller was snoring within minutes, but Sairy lay there, listening to the night sounds.

In the loft, Dallas closed his eyes. Immediately, a long-ago trio appeared, as if they were sneaking out from behind a curtain and taking their turn on stage. Floating across his mind's stage were Mr. and Mrs. Cranbep and their daughter, Gigi, with her curly yellow hair.

Dallas and Florida were seven when they went to live with the Cranbeps. "You're so lucky," Mrs. Cranbep had told them. "To be with us now and to have a new sister like Gigi."

At night, Gigi would come into Dallas and Florida's room and spit on them. One night, after Gigi spit on him, Dallas punched her in the stomach.

"You stupid brute," Mrs. Cranbep said to him. "Beating on a little girl! If you ever touch her again, you'll be out of here so fast your head will spin."

The next night, Gigi came into their room and skipped over to Florida's bed. "Your hair is stupid," she told Florida as she tugged it.

"Quit it, you little cockroach," Florida said. "That hurts."

Gigi pulled so hard that pieces of Florida's hair came away in her hands. Later that night, Florida snuck into Gigi's room and gathered up all of Gigi's dolls.

"Wake up, Dallas," she said. "You and me have got some hair-pulling to do."

When the Cranbeps returned Florida and Dallas to the Boxton Creek Home, Mrs. Cranbep emptied a bag of bald dolls onto the Trepids' desk. "These twins are *demented*," Mrs. Cranbep said.

"Dallas?" Florida whispered. "You think we should go now? You think they're alseep?"

"Shh," Dallas said. He sat up and reached for his boots. "I guess they're asleep by now. I guess they won't hear us." But he stayed where he was, as if he were stuck to the bed.

Florida sat on the bed opposite, facing him. "I wonder what they'll think when they see that we've hit the grit."

"Shh—don't talk like that. They probably won't think anything."

Florida smoothed the quilt on the bed, licked her finger, and rubbed at a spot on the quilt. "You don't think they'll have giganza heart attacks or something, do you? You don't think the shock will scare them to death, do you?"

"Aww, shoot," Dallas said. "What'd you go and say that for? That idea wasn't even in my head till you said it."

"Forget it," Florida said. "They'll probably be relieved. They'll probably be glad they don't have to cook for us anymore. They'll be glad they don't have to cart us along with them on their trips. They'll probably have a celebration. They'll probably—"

"Enough already," Dallas said. "If we're going, we better get moving."

"What? Now?"

"Now."

24

Tiller and Sairy

Tiller's eyes were tightly closed, but he wasn't yet asleep. He was willing himself to dream about his trip to the Rutabago River. He could do that sometimes, make himself dream about a certain thing. Usually he tried to do it when he had a problem, in hopes that the dream would help him sort it out.

The first time he'd done it was when their second child, Lucy, was a toddler. Lucy went through a terrible sick spell, listless and pale for weeks on end. The doctor ran tests, so many tests, so many punctures in the little girl's arms, so many tubes hooked here and there. When the tests were finished, Tiller and Sairy took Lucy home to await the results. As they were leaving the hospital, Tiller said, "But she won't eat anything except Popsicles, orange Popsicles. What should we feed her?"

"Let her eat Popsicles," the doctor said. "No harm in that."

That night, Tiller made himself dream about Lucy so he could figure out what was wrong with her. In his dream, Lucy was lying on a cot, holding a dripping orange Popsicle. The orange drips turned to red, like blood, and made terrible sizzling noises when they touched her skin. "Ow, Daddy, the Popsicle hurts," Lucy told Tiller in his dream.

When Tiller awoke the next morning, he threw away all the orange Popsicles. Then he filled a pot with well water, and began tossing in the ingredients for getting-better soup, making up the recipe as he went along. Tiller told Lucy that all the Popsicles had disappeared in the night, but in their place, an angel had brought Lucy Soup, only for Lucy, not for Buddy or Tiller or Sairy. Lucy took a tentative sip. Then another. And another. When she finished the first bowl, she asked for a second helping. By evening, she was chasing Buddy out on the porch. By the next morning, she was racing to the creek, her cheeks pink, her little arms flapping beside her like wings.

When Tiller returned, alone, to the doctor's office the following week, the doctor apologized. "The tests were inconclusive," he said. "We'll need to do more tests."

"No we won't," Tiller said. "It was Popsicles. Orange Popsicles. She must be allergic to them."

The doctor was scornful. "I don't think—"

"Trust me," Tiller said. "Orange Popsicles."

Now, as he lay in bed in the cabin, thinking about his trip to the mighty Rutabago River, he again asked his mind to dream. This time he hoped the dream would tell him whether he should take the trip or not. He was feeling anxious about leaving Sairy, and nervous about being responsible for Florida. Would he have enough patience?

ᎧᎧ

Beside him, Sairy was also still awake, and she, too, was fretting over her upcoming trip. For so long she had dreamed of taking a trip by herself, without Tiller. She had been with him nearly all of her life, and she wanted to see if she were different when she was alone. Would she think different things? Do different things? Who was she, all by herself?

She drifted off to sleep, but when Tiller's snoring woke her, she got up and went into the living room and opened the trunk in the corner. In it were bits and pieces of her past: on top were their grown children's wedding photos and, beneath those, drawings from when the children were young, and farther down she found a photo of herself when she was nineteen, standing in front of a café, in New York City.

Sairy peered at her younger self, with her long dark hair and her smooth skin. She had gone to New York to attend college, so excited, so eager for all the sounds and smells of that busy city. She'd been there two weeks when Tiller appeared at her door.

"I decided to come, too," he said. "I missed you."

"You can't," she told him. "Go home."

"Home?" he said. "I want to be here with you. I'm going to get a job and—"

"Not here you aren't," Sairy said. "Go home."

She closed the door on him and stood there, angry at first, and then mortified at what she had done. He had looked so stunned, standing there.

A week later, a postcard came from Ruby Holler. On it, Tiller had written, "The maples are blazing rubies."

The next week, another postcard: "The maples have turned to gold, and willow leaves float along the creek."

On Tiller went like that, sending a postcard every week for the next six months, each with a note about what was happening in Ruby Holler: how the first snow sifted down, how an ice storm left millions of diamonds dazzling in the trees, hundreds of little sentences about the place she had left, and nothing about himself.

By spring, Sairy had grown increasingly agitated by the loud noises of the city, with the screeching trucks and blaring horns and pounding jackhammers. The smells of the city, which had at first delighted her, began to assault her: sausages and doughnuts, tar and urine, gasoline and sewage. When she received Tiller's postcard about the first purple crocuses springing up beside the creek and new leaves dangling like emeralds, she packed her bags and moved back to Ruby Holler.

And there in the trunk in the cabin, beneath the picture of Sairy in New York City, was a photo of Tiller and Sairy on their wedding day. She looked closely at Tiller's smooth skin, that tall, straight back, that engaging grin. She stared at her younger self. *Who are you inside there?* she asked Sairy-in-the-photo.

Sairy closed the trunk. Maybe these trips they were planning *were* foolish. She crossed the room to the loft ladder, listening. Aside from Tiller's occasional snores, it was awfully quiet in the cabin tonight.

∾ 25 ∾

The Holler
at Night

Ruby Holler at night can be an eerie, dark place, full of shadows and silence, but both the shadows and the silence are deceptive. Out of the shadows dash creatures of all shapes and sizes: swift, diving bats and scurrying raccoons, fluttery moths and cunning bobcats. From the deepest silence erupt groans and howls, snorts and squawks, creaks and croaks. Paths, which in daylight seem clearly trodden ways, twist and turn in the night, looping back on themselves and vanishing into dense thickets. Out of nowhere, boulders loom, and fallen trees barricade the way. Roots and holes and swampy earth snare unsuspecting feet.

Into this dark, dense maze stumbled Florida and Dallas. Barely ten minutes from the cabin, they were tangled in a thicket.

"What's this stupid bush doing here?" Florida grumbled. "It wasn't here before. What'd you go this way for?"

"Must've gotten turned around," Dallas said. "Sure is dark out here."

"I've hardly ever seen anything so dark," Florida said.

"What about that cellar at that scary toothless lunatic's house?" Dallas asked.

"That trapdoor cellar? With the lizards and the rats? Mighty dark. Mighty, mighty, mighty dark." Florida thrashed and kicked and tugged her way out of the thicket. She hated thinking about the scary toothless lunatic's house, but once it was in her mind, it raced around in there, bashing up against every little bulging gray cell.

When the scary toothless man, Mr. Dreep, and his thin, fidgety wife first came to the Home, Dallas and Florida had instantly feared the man and tried their best to dissuade the couple from any interest in them.

"We're loud and messy," Florida said.

"And clumsy klutzes," Dallas offered.

Mr. Dreep stared at them while his wife's fingers twirled nervously in her lap. Mr. Trepid sat to one side clucking his tongue.

"They're no louder or messier than any other kids," Mr. Trepid said. "And they're very strong for their age."

Mr. Dreep nodded. "Aye," he said.

"We're stupid," Florida said. "I can't even read."

"Of course she can read," Mr. Trepid said.

"Can't," Florida said. "Try me. Give me any old thing, and I'll bet you I can't read it."

"It's true," Dallas said. "She can't read. And me, heck, I can't remember hardly anything from one minute to the next. You tell me to do something, and shoot, I'll forget what you said before you finish saying it."

But Dallas and Florida had been forced to go along with Mr. and Mrs. Dreep, and all the way to the Dreeps' home, no one spoke in the car, and no one spoke until they'd pulled up in front of a falling-down house with broken windows and a sagging porch and holes in the roof.

"I'm not staying here," Florida said.

Mr. Dreep opened the back door and pulled Florida out. "Yes, you are," he said. He turned to Mrs. Dreep, whose fingers were playing a little melody on her neck. "Okay," Mr. Dreep said to his wife. "You wanted kids. You got kids."

They'd been inside only a few minutes when Mr. Dreep said, "Got a well that needs digging. That's your job, tomorrow."

"You're kidding, right?" Florida said. "People don't dig wells. Machines do."

"We don't have any machines," Mr. Dreep said. "We got you two."

"Sorry, sir," Dallas said, "but we are not able to dig you a well."

"Are you sassing me?" Mr. Dreep said. "Here's the first rule in this house: no sassing. Got that?" Mr. Dreep lifted a trapdoor to the cellar and said, "Go on, have a look. There's some neat stuff down there."

Dallas started down the ladder, with Florida after him. The door closed over them, and a lock clicked. It was pitch black, so dark that Dallas and Florida couldn't see each other although they were barely a foot apart. Something skittered across Dallas's foot.

It was terrible in the cellar, all night long, all the cold, damp night long with the rats and lizards and bugs and wretched smells.

Now, lost in the holler, Florida said to Dallas, "You don't think there's any rats out here, do you?"

Dallas peered into the black gloom. "What'd you go and say that for? Quit talking about rats."

"I just don't want any whiskery disgusting thing gnawing at my legs, is all," Florida said.

"Quit talking about it. I'm not listening. Whoa! What was that? You see that?"

Florida covered her head with her hands. "Some flying rat sort of thing."

On they went through the holler, stumbling, tripping, falling, scrambling. Through soggy patches, over rocks and across a stream, sliding down banks and whacking through brush.

"We don't have any dang idea where we are, do we?" Florida demanded. "We might be in the lost wilderness—in the lost, lost, lost wilderness where nobody's ever been and nobody's going to get out alive."

"I don't get it," Dallas said. "It's like somebody came out here and moved everything around, just to mess us up."

"You got any idea whatsoever where that train passes by?" Florida said.

"I got an idea—"

"But is it a right idea?"

"I don't exactly know if it's a right idea," Dallas said, "but it's an idea."

"Well, I think we ought to stop," Florida said. "We might be going in circles. We might be going to the lostest place ever. We might—"

"Okay. We'll stop. We'll camp here. We've got sleeping bags, right? We'll just sleep a couple hours," Dallas said.

"Then when it's starting to get light—just a wee little bit—we'll know where we are," Florida said.

They spread their sleeping bags on the ground and hurried inside them.

"Dallas? We're going to miss the train, right?"

"You got rocks under your sleeping bag? I've got rocks under mine," Dallas said. He stared up into the blackness overhead. "I guess we might miss that train tonight. But that's okay. We'll just get the one tomorrow night."

"I wish we could zip these things right over our heads," Florida said. "I wish there wasn't this hole at the top. Any old rat thing could crawl inside."

"Not listening."

An hour later, Dallas said, "Stupid rocks. I can't sleep. You asleep, Florida?"

"No. Things are crawling around my head."

"Let's talk about something," Dallas said. "Keep our minds off the rocks and crawly things. Tell me about that river journey. What did you and Tiller plan?"

Florida sat up and pulled her sleeping bag tightly around her. "Well," she said, "we were going to haul the boat down to where the creek turns into Hidden River— "

"How were you going to do that?" Dallas asked.

"Tiller knows some guy with a trailer."

"And then what? You put it in the river and off you go—paddling or rowing or what?"

"Paddling."

"What? Paddling like crazy, day and night?"

"Naw," Florida said. "The current would mostly take us down the river, and then we got that little motor in case we get tired or in case we run into trouble somewhere."

"What kind of trouble?" Dallas asked.

"I don't know, that's just what Tiller said. Maybe some big calm stretch or maybe if we both broke our arms or something."

Dallas had climbed out of his sleeping bag and was picking rocks out of the dirt and sailing them into the brush. "So on down the river you go, and then what? How do you know where you're going?"

"It's a river. It just goes. Then it turns into other rivers: the Goochee River and then the Mackalack River, on and on, a bazillion little rivers and creeks. We got maps and all, to see where the little towns are and to find places to tie up and stuff like that. And then we hit the mighty Rutabago."

"I bet that's a sight to see," Dallas said.

"Must be," Florida said, "if Tiller wants to leave this holler so bad to go find it." Florida scooted out of her sleeping bag and started helping Dallas clear rocks. She felt odd talking about the trip now that she wasn't going on it. She wanted to stop talking about it.

"What about that trip to Kangadoon?" she said. "Tell me about that."

"First, we were going to get a ride to the airport," Dallas said, "and get on a plane—a real plane, you know? One of those jet things. And fly, fly, fly—"

"What? Like over the ocean?"

"Fly right out over the ocean," Dallas said, "and land on a tiny island, *wham! Kangadoon!* And then hike, hike, hike and search, search, search for the red-tailed rocking bird. Hey, I have a picture of that bird. Want to see it?"

"What? Here?"

Dallas rummaged through his backpack. "In here somewhere . . ." He retrieved a flashlight and a pamphlet and pointed to a picture on the back.

"What a funny-looking thing," Florida said. "Little chicken body and that long lopsided tail and all those different colors. It looks like it rolled around in a zillion paint pots."

Dallas stared at the picture. "Don't you

wonder why Sairy would want to go all the way to Kangadoon to find this funny-looking bird, when there are funny-looking birds all over the holler?"

"Maybe they're both losing their brains a little bit," Florida said.

Dallas snatched at the pamphlet and stuffed it deep into his backpack. "We'd better quit talking and get some sleep," he grumbled.

"You don't have to get so grouchy," Florida said.

"I'm not grouchy. I'm just tired. Go to sleep."

"Yes sir, Mr. Boss, but you'd better remember one thing. I don't like being bossed around so much." She slipped back into her sleeping bag and scooted down inside as far as she could. "If a rat thing gets me, I hope you'll beat it to death," she said.

"Not listening."

Florida tried counting to put herself to sleep. *Four hundred and three, four hundred and four, stupid numbers, stupid night.* She turned onto her stomach, and as soon as she did so, she thought about the Burgertons.

She and Dallas were eight when they went to live with the Burgertons. "You must always sleep on your stomach," Mrs. Burgerton had said. "It isn't healthy to sleep on your back."

Dallas and Florida thought that was a strange thing, but they slept on their stomachs so as not to get in trouble. At least they *tried* to sleep on their stomachs. They couldn't help it if their sleeping bodies automatically turned over in the night. Mrs. Burgerton would come into their rooms while they were sleeping and flip them back over on their stomachs. "Can't you remember anything?" she'd say.

But except for that, and for Mrs. Burgerton's insistence that Florida and Dallas dress alike ("Like twins!"), Mr. and Mrs. Burgerton seemed nicer to them than other people had been, and more patient, too.

"Maybe they'll keep us," Dallas had told Florida.

And then the Burgertons' sons came home from summer camp. The three Burgerton boys were tall and thin and pale, and they were none too thrilled to find the twins taking up space in their house.

The Burgerton boys threw rocks through the garage window and told their parents that Dallas had done it. They set fire to the neighbor's playhouse and blamed Florida. The boys told Dallas and Florida that if they tattled, their tongues would be chopped up into tiny bits.

One afternoon, Dallas and Forida gathered up dozens of ants, seven spiders, two garter snakes, and a frog, and that evening they deposited these treasures in the beds of the Burgerton boys.

"If we're going to get blamed for everything," Florida had told Dallas, "we might as well actually *do* something to get blamed for."

When the Burgertons took Dallas and Florida back to the Boxton Creek Home, Dallas and Florida were relieved.

"We were lucky to get out of there alive," Dallas told Florida.

"I know it," Florida said.

Shack Talk

It was dark in Boxton, and Mr. Trepid was in his hideaway shack in the alley. With him was a man who was known only as Z. Mr. Trepid thought of Z as a shiftless man, slipping in and out of town like a slithery possum.

Mr. Trepid did not like either the smell of the man or the looks of him: the matted hair, shiny with grease; the rumpled, frayed clothes, thick with grime; the cloudy green eyes behind their half-closed lids. But what he did like about Z was that Z would do whatever Mr. Trepid asked him to do, as long as money was involved.

Mr. Trepid did not know where Z lived, nor did he want to know. He wanted to know as little as possible about the man. On this cool summer night, all he wanted to know was if Z could get him some information and if he could take on a project down in the holler.

"Depends," Z said, "on what I gotta do and how hard I gotta work to do it." He slid his fingers through his gnarled hair, tugging at a knot. "And it depends on the, er, er—"

"I know, I know," Mr. Trepid said. "The salary." He pulled a wad of bills out of his pocket. "Now this here is for the first part— finding out when they're leaving town. That should be simple enough." Mr. Trepid shoved the bills at Z.

Z looked over the money. "I don't know about it being so simple."

Mr. Trepid shoved more money at Z. "There. I'm sure that will be quite enough for your efforts."

Z smiled, and as he did so, Mr. Trepid turned away from the crooked teeth.

"What about the second part?" Z asked. "The surveying part? And what is it exactly I gotta survey?"

"When you get me the first part of the information, we will discuss the second part in more detail." Mr. Trepid opened the door, indicating that it was time for Z to leave.

"Whatever you say, boss," Z said, and he slipped out of the door, down the alley, and across the railroad tracks, disappearing into the trees on the far side.

When Mr. Trepid was sure that Z was gone, he closed the door of the shack and paced inside, back and forth across its tiny interior. He pressed his fingers to his lips. *An adventure,* he thought. *An adventure in Ruby Holler.*

✪ 27 ✪

Trials

Burrowed deep inside her sleeping bag, Florida wondered if it was morning yet. Her stomach felt like a pitiful empty sack. She'd been hungry last night when they were scrabbling through the woods, and she'd been hungry when they stopped for the night, but she'd been afraid to mention it because she hadn't remembered to pack any food. What if that had been her job, to pack the food?

Dallas was twisted upside down in his sleeping bag. He'd gotten out of it in the night and crawled in headfirst and then twisted the opening around his feet. He figured that if any rat things tried to get him, they'd have to get his feet first, and he'd wake up if that happened, and he'd be able to kick those rat things. He didn't want them messing with his face.

Lord, he was hungry, hungry, hungry. It was a bad thing, he decided, getting used to all that good food that Sairy and Tiller heaped on the table. Now it was all he could think of. Before he'd come to Sairy and Tiller's, he'd been able to go a couple of days without food. You just turned your stomach off. You turned your brain off. You moved a little slower. But now he was hungry, hungry, hungry, and he was mad at himself for forgetting to pack food, and he was wondering when Florida was going to mention it.

When Florida heard Dallas moving around, she unwrapped her head and blinked at the soft gray light sifting down through a gap in the leaves overhead. She loved the smell out here, of earth and bark and pine and . . . and . . . what was that other smell? That delicious smell?

She leaped out of her sleeping bag as Dallas came out of his feetfirst.

"Dallas!"

He was ready for her. "I know, I know, don't

start on me," he said. "The reason I didn't pack any food was because—"

"Dallas, take a whiff—what do you smell?"

He sniffed. "Trees. I smell trees and—hey! What's that other smell?"

Florida inhaled deeply. "Either I'm out of my noodle or else that's bacon I smell, Dallas. *Bacon*."

"It can't be bacon," Dallas said. "It must be something that smells like bacon, and I wish it didn't because it's made my stomach wake up, and my stomach is saying it wants food right now, right this minute." He sniffed the air again. "It does smell an awful lot like bacon. Maybe it's some old codger who's living in the woods and he's making his breakfast."

"And maybe," Florida said, "it's some convict who'd just as soon shoot us as feed us."

"Why'd you go and say that?"

"'Cause it might be true. Let's be real quiet."

They set off through the trees, slowly, quietly. The smell of frying bacon drew them on, closer, closer.

Out of the brush came a booming "Hey there!"

Dallas and Florida leaped toward each other.

"Tiller?" Dallas said. "Is that you, Tiller, or am I dreaming?"

"Howdy, kids. Didn't mean to scare you. I was just out here getting more kindling for the fire. Follow me."

Tiller led them through a clump of bushes and there, on the other side, was Sairy, seated on a flat gray stone, her hand stretched toward a big black skillet full of bacon.

"There you are," she said. "Mornin'."

Florida leaned toward Dallas. "We're dreaming, right? We died in the middle of the night and now we're dead and our dead brains are dreaming, right?"

Sairy handed her tongs to Tiller so that he could take over the frying of the bacon. "You two are about the smartest kids I ever met," she said. "Coming up with such a good idea, to try out our equipment before we set off on our trips. I don't know why we didn't think of that ourselves, do you, Tiller?"

"Erm—"

"But how'd you know we were gone, and

how'd you know where we were?" Dallas said.
"How'd you find us?"

"I couldn't sleep," Sairy said, "and so I went
up to check on you, like I do every night—"

"You've been checking on us every night?"
Florida said.

Sairy looked sheepish. "It's just a mother
thing," she said. "Kids in the house, I check on
'em. When I saw you were gone, I figured you
must've decided to try out these sleeping bags
and stuff. I thought that was the most brilliant
idea. So me and Tiller, we decided to join you."

"But how'd you find us?" Florida said. "I
mean, not that we were hiding or anything,
but—"

"Sairy has a nose for where kids go," Tiller
said.

"And then," Sairy said, "when we saw
where you were camping, we went back and
got some food and the skillet, because we knew
we'd all be hungry this morning. Ready to eat?"

Tiller passed around tin plates, which Sairy
heaped with eggs and bacon and warm biscuits.
"Anyone want honey?" Sairy asked.

Accepting a generous spoonful, Dallas said, "I suppose we should have told you we were going—"

"—out in the woods," Florida said. "To try out our things, like you said. We probably should have told you."

"No call to do that," Sairy said. "I can see what you were thinking. You were thinking, *Let's not disturb Tiller and Sairy. Let's just try out this stuff without bothering anybody.* Kids ought to have a little choice, that's what I think. They ought to be able to do stuff without someone watching over their shoulders every minute."

Florida licked the honey from her fingers. "Well, ma'am, that's a mighty interesting way to think."

"So," Sairy said, "what's the verdict? Think those sleeping bags work okay?"

"Well," Florida said, "we think maybe the sleeping bags should have some sort of thing over the head part."

"Like what?" Tiller asked.

"Something to keep out the crawly bugs."

"Ah," Sairy said. "Now that's a brilliant observation. We've got some mosquito netting, and I could sew some of that around the top, find some way to fasten it so you could open and close it."

Tiller waved his hand in the air. "You're not going to make it too loopy and fancy, are you? I don't want a bunch of lace or anything around my head."

"Maybe you won't have anything whatsoever around your head," Sairy said. "Maybe we'll let the bugs get you." She turned to Dallas and Florida. "Anything else you think of while you were trying out the equipment?"

"Yeah," Dallas said. "I was thinking we ought to be sure and have enough food—you know, in case we get stuck somewhere, or lost or—"

"Yep," Tiller agreed. "I can't hardly think without food in my stomach. We didn't plan too much about food yet."

"I'm sure glad you two had the genius idea to make this trial run," Sairy added.

"Aw," Florida said, "it was nothin'."

ೲ

While Dallas and Florida went back to get their sleeping bags, Tiller and Sairy packed up the breakfast things.

"Well," Tiller said. "How'd I do?"

"You did fine," Sairy said.

"Only because I kept my mouth pretty much closed."

"Keeps you out of trouble," Sairy said.

"I guess you were right," he said. "They weren't out here stealing our money, like I thought."

"Of course they weren't."

"And I guess you were right, too, about them running away."

Sairy stood with her hands on her hips. "I don't know what got into them, I really don't. Are you sure you didn't say anything to scare them off?"

"I've been on my best behavior, honest," Tiller said.

"I'm just glad we found them. I don't know what I'd have done if we hadn't." Sairy pressed her hand against the middle of her back. "Sleeping on the ground isn't so easy anymore, is it?"

"Nope," Tiller said.

Sairy gathered up the pans. "Now look, Tiller, you be extra nice to those kids, you hear?"

Tiller bowed. "Yes ma'am, whatever you say."

"I mean it."

"I know you do," he said. "And I will try my best to become Mr. Personality."

ᔆᔆ 28 ᔆᔆ

Mrs. Trepid

Mrs. Trepid was standing by her bedroom window, staring at two empty trash cans rolling against the curb. *Clank, clank, clank.* She wished someone would pick up those cans and stop that annoying noise. *Clank, clank, clank.*

A young woman walked past, her arms swinging loosely, oblivious to the clanking trash cans. *Look at her,* Mrs. Trepid thought, *walking along without a care in the world.* She wanted to throw something at the woman, to jolt her out of her little dream world.

Mrs. Trepid's gaze shifted to the porch below. It was on that same porch that the twins had first appeared in a box. She'd even seen the woman who left them. From this very window where she stood now, Mrs. Trepid had spotted the woman, bundled in a tattered and faded green dress, bending over the box. The woman had leaned down so close to the box, and then she had rushed down the walk, her hands pressed to her face.

And then Morgan called up the stairs to say that it was babies in the box, two babies. *Twins!*

Mrs. Trepid talked her husband into ripping up the forms they were supposed to submit to the authorities, reporting the twins' arrival. "Let's not tell, yet," she said. "Maybe these could be *our* babies." The more she thought about that, the more she feared that the woman in the tattered green dress would return and claim them. When Mrs. Trepid was out walking the babies in the buggy, she was always watching, terrified that the woman would appear and snatch the twins away.

When people came to the Home to meet the other children, Mrs. Trepid tried to keep the twins hidden. Once, when a couple saw the twins and inquired about them, Mrs. Trepid said, "They're already taken."

Even as infants, Florida was the squirmy one, and Dallas the quieter, dreamier one. Mrs. Trepid was intrigued by the way they clung to each other, and the way they responded to each other's gurgles, and the way they reached for each other when they were separated. *Two babies who came into the world at the same time.* Sometimes Mrs. Trepid felt a little jealous of them. *They'll always have each other. They'll always have one person who understands them completely.*

At first Mrs. Trepid didn't want Morgan or Mr. Trepid to help care for the twins. She wanted to do it all herself. But she had so little patience, and always one of them needed attention, and she hated when they howled and squirmed. So much trouble every single day.

She started wishing the woman in the tattered green dress *would* come back and claim her twins. After one particularly trying day, Mrs. Trepid snared her husband. "File the forms!" she ordered. "Tell the authorities that these twin kids just arrived and are available!"

To her surpise, though, people were wary of taking on twins. "Twins?" they'd say. "Who would want to take two at once? Lovely idea, but no thanks."

By the time the twins were toddlers, Mrs. Trepid couldn't bear their stumbling and falling and screaming and banging and breaking and spitting. Everything they did was louder and messier than what other kids did, or at least that's how it seemed to Mrs. Trepid.

Now, as she stood at the window looking down on the street, Mrs. Trepid thought about all the long years ahead and wondered how she could live through more children and more running and spitting and banging and leaving.

Clank, clank, clank. The garbage cans bashed against the curb below.

Mrs. Trepid leaned out the window. "Somebody pick those up!" she pleaded. "They're driving me crazy."

Decisions

Dallas, Florida, Tiller, and Sairy had packed up the breakfast things and retrieved the sleeping bags and returned to the cabin, and now Dallas and Florida were out running through the hills.

"Go on," Sairy had urged. "You two need a day off from work. Why don't you go run awhile?"

"Holler a bit, too, while you're at it," Tiller said. "I like to hear a bit of hollering in the holler every now and then."

"Most people don't like hollering," Florida said. "Some people would lock us up in a cobwebby basement for hollering."

"Tell you what," Tiller said. "If I ever lose my brains and lock you up somewhere, you bust out and then you—you bite me and kick me and tie me up and throw me over the cliff, y'hear?"

"Okay," Dallas said. "If you ever lock us up, that's what we'll do."

So Dallas and Florida had run down the hill and sloshed through the creek, and then they ran up the opposite hill, and on top of it they whooped and hollered. And when they were tired of hollering they flopped down in the dirt.

"So what do you think, Dallas? What's our plan now?"

Dallas scratched at the dirt with a stick. "What do you think our plan should be?" he asked.

"Well, I've been thinking that these old people—this Tiller and Sairy—they've got their hearts set on finding the mighty Rutabago and zinging over to Kangadoon to see that rocking-thing bird. And I've been thinking that maybe—now, I'm just saying maybe—I'm not saying for certain sure—maybe it wouldn't hurt us all that much to go on their trips with them, and—"

"—then when we got back, we could still catch that night train," Dallas said.

"That's right," Florida said. "That's what I've been thinking. Is that what you've been thinking, too?"

"Pretty much," Dallas said.

"Even though we promised never, never, ever to split up."

"This would be an exception."

"Like a once-and-only exception," Florida said.

"Right," Dallas agreed. "When we get back, it'll be just like before, and we'll stay together and nobody will split us up." He was picturing himself on the beach, building a hut and eating coconuts.

"Guess we ought to bury our money again," Florida said.

Tiller and Sairy were sitting on the porch swing.

"Are you going to miss me?" Sairy asked.

"Of course I'm going to miss you," Tiller

said. "How could I not miss you? You've been right here most of the days of my life."

"That makes me sound like an old sock."

Tiller turned to look at his wife. He knew every line on her face, every expression. Sometimes he felt he knew everything about her, maybe more than he knew about himself. He felt light-headed and weak and had to press his hand against his chest to ease the sudden fluttering inside. "Are you going to miss me?" he said.

She turned to him. "You feel alright?"

"Sure," he said. "Sure I do."

Sairy slipped her arm through his. She wondered what it would be like to be among complete strangers, with people who didn't know anything about her and who didn't expect her to be a certain way. "Of course I'll miss you," she said. "You're like an old comfortable boot."

"An old, comfortable, *handsome* boot," Tiller said. He closed his eyes and imagined the winding river. "Will you miss the holler?"

Sairy looked out across the hillside, down

toward the creek. "If you'd asked me that last month, I'd have said no, but lately, the holler seems more like the enchanting place it used to be. Strange, isn't it?"

Tiller had felt the same way, but he was surprised to hear Sairy say it. "So you *are* coming back, then? You're not going to decide to stay on that island out in the ocean with your what's-it bird?"

"You old boot," she said. "Of course I'm coming back. And you are, too."

"Maybe," he said. "Or maybe I'll like being on the river so much that I'll just go on and on—"

"Cut that out."

"We could cancel our trips, you know," Tiller said.

"Naw. Those kids are counting on these trips. It would be a shame to disappoint them."

∾ 30 ∾

Nightmares

That night, wind whipped through the holler in relentless surges, howling through the trees and rattling window-panes. Thunder boomed and lightning cracked, lighting up the sky in sudden, glaring washes.

"Dallas?" Florida whispered. "It sure is loud out there."

"It's just thunder," he said.

"Dallas? I had a terrible nightmare. I dreamed I was upside down in a boat, under the water, and I couldn't get out."

"Go back to sleep," he said. "Don't think about it." He promptly rolled over and drifted back to sleep, returning to the clear creek he'd left when Florida had woken him. But now a huge wind was whipping the creek and the waves were getting taller and taller, and one giant wave swept him backward over the bank, over a hill, into a jungle, and the wave kept pushing him farther and farther into a tangled mess of trees.

Downstairs, Tiller was thrashing in his sleep. He was all alone in the middle of a river, and the boat was sinking, sinking, sinking.

Sairy sat up with a start. She heard the thunder boom and the wind rage around the house. *Oh, whew,* she thought. *It was only a dream.* She settled back against her pillow, trying to forget her dream, in which a red-tailed bird had turned into a dinosaur and was lunging toward her.

∽ 31 ∽

Medicine

At breakfast, Sairy said, "Everybody's a little quiet this morning."

"Uh-huh," Tiller said.

Florida swallowed a mouthful of waffle. "That was a putrid storm last night," she said. "I had some mighty awful nightmares."

"Why, me too," Sairy said. "I got attacked by a red-tailed dinosaur."

"You did?" Florida said. "I got trapped by a boat, underwater."

"My boat sank," Tiller said, "with me in it."

"I got pushed by a wave into a jungle with man-eating rats," Dallas said.

"Hmm," Sairy said. "Looks like we need a

little bad-dream medicine."

"Medicine?" Florida said. "Don't want any stinking medicine."

"You might like this kind," Sairy said, retrieving a tub of freshly made peach ice cream. "Goes good with waffles," she said.

"Ice cream?" Dallas said. "For breakfast?"

"Erases nightmares," Tiller explained. "Works every time."

After breakfast, when they were clearing fallen branches from the porch, Tiller said, "I had a crazy notion just now."

"Nothing new about that," Sairy said.

"Very funny," Tiller said. "Do you want to hear my notion or not?"

"You're going to tell us anyway, I bet," Sairy said.

"You're awful feisty this morning," Tiller said.

"Go on," Sairy said. "Tell us your crazy notion."

"Naw, it's too stupid."

"Tell us," Florida said. "Even if it's stupid, tell us."

"Okay," Tiller said. "I had this crazy notion that maybe we all ought to have some rehearsals."

"What sort of rehearsals?" Dallas asked. "Like for a play? We don't know how to do plays and stuff."

"No, not a play. You know how you kids went out and had a trial run with our equipment? Well, like that, only this time, it'd be me and Florida trying out our boat. Just a little close-by kind of trip. A day or two or three. And Dallas and Sairy could take a trial hike since they're going to have to hike so much when they get to Kangadoon. They could hike out of the holler, camp somewhere, hike some more, you know, try out the boots and tents and compasses and stuff. Crazy notion, huh?"

Everyone else was quiet. Dallas was remembering the huge wave and the rat-filled jungle. Florida was thinking about being caught under the boat, and Sairy was recalling the red-tailed dinosaur.

"Maybe not so crazy," Florida said. "Not so entirely crazy."

"Maybe not crazy at all," Dallas said.

Sairy leaned against Tiller. "Maybe it's a tiny little genius idea."

"Genius?" Tiller said. "Me?"

"Don't you go getting a big head," Sairy said. "I said maybe it was a tiny little genius *idea*. That's all I said."

∾ 32 ∾

Paddling and Hiking

The air was heavy and hot, and the clear water of the Hidden River was smooth and still.

"How long have we been slapping these paddles in the water?" Florida asked. "About eighty gazillion hours?"

"Four hours," Tiller said. "You tired? You stop paddling when you're tired. I can carry on back here."

"I've never paddled a boat before," Florida said.

"Is that right?" Tiller said. "I wouldn't have guessed that."

Florida turned around to look at Tiller. His

straw hat shaded his eyes and made crisscross marks on the upper half of his face. "I know you're not telling the truth," Florida said. "I know you were getting a bit troubled when we first started off and I couldn't get the hang of this paddle thing and nearly tipped us over a hundred times."

"It takes a little time to get the feel of a boat," Tiller said. "I wasn't doing so hot myself when we first set off." He gazed at the banks and at the sky overhead. He'd wanted to turn back a hundred times. *What am I doing here?* he kept asking himself.

"How come this is called Hidden River?" Florida asked.

"'Cause it's not on any map, at least not any map I've ever seen," Tiller said.

"How'd you know it was here then?"

"My father and I found it. I've been down here many times, and I know right where it goes," Tiller said.

"Then how come it's not on a map?"

Tiller shrugged. "Not everything is on maps."

"Well, if this river that is here is not on a

map, how do you know that the rivers that *are* on the maps are really there?"

"We don't know, not exactly. Guess we'll find out," Tiller said.

"You mean we might end up in a dried-up smelly ditch someplace and be lost and maybe starve to death in a lost place that nobody knows about, and—"

"I think we'll be okay," he said. *She sure has a lot of questions,* he thought. *Why didn't I just come by myself?* "You've got to admit, this is mighty peaceful," he said.

Florida stared ahead at the river, a long sparkly slithery thing disappearing around a bend in the distance. "It's peaceful alright," Florida said, "except for these dang mosquitoes and flies." She slapped at her arms. "How come there are so many bugs out here?"

"Probably no bats around these parts," Tiller said.

"Bats?"

"You ever notice all those bats in the holler, the ones that come out at dusk?"

"Those flying rat things?" Florida said.

"Those are bats," Tiller said. "You ever notice how there aren't any mosquitoes in Ruby Holler?"

"Now that you mention it, I did notice that," Florida said. "How come you don't have mosquitoes in Ruby Holler?"

"Because of the bats," Tiller said. "The bats eat them. Bats are good."

"Well, I never would have guessed that any flying rat thing could be good," Florida said. "But I'll take your word for it. Maybe you could whistle for some of those bats to follow us on our trip. You think Sairy and Dallas have bats where they are?"

"No idea," Tiller said. "Where do you suppose they are right now? How far do you think they've hiked?"

Florida felt quivery talking about Sairy and Dallas. It had been awful saying good-bye that morning. Tiller's friend had driven them all down to the river, where they'd unloaded the boat and plonked it in the water, and then Tiller's friend was going to drive Sairy and

Dallas back to the cabin so they could set off on their hike. Florida had had an odd feeling when she met Tiller's friend, as if she'd seen him somewhere before, but she couldn't place where that might have been.

They'd all stood around looking at the boat bobbing in the water until Sairy said, "I can't hardly take all this standing around. I'm going to bust out blubbering." In a tangle, they'd exchanged hugs, and Tiller and Florida stood on the bank waving good-bye.

It was all Florida could do not to chase after Dallas and flee. Everything inside her head told her not to trust anybody but him. She had a sudden, cold fear that this was all a trick, a plot to separate her from Dallas. She was mad at herself for letting Tiller and Sairy soften them up with their good food and gentle ways.

Still, something had made her get in the boat, and something had made her dip her paddle in the water, and something had made her look calm on the outside, while inside she was trembling like a trapped mouse.

☙☙

It had taken two hours for Dallas and Sairy to hike beyond the limits of the holler, and now they stood on top of a ridge, looking back the way they'd come.

"There's a river," Dallas said. "See it? Looks like a skinny brown eel. Is that Hidden River? Will we be able to see them down there, you think? Look at all those tiny houses and cars and that skinny river. It's like a playland. It's like your carvings."

Sairy stared off across the hills. "Dallas, did you ever wonder what you were like without Florida?"

"How do you mean?"

Sairy took off her hat and rumpled her hair. "I mean, you two have always been together, your whole lives, but did you ever wonder if you'd be different if you weren't with her, if you were by yourself?"

Dallas kicked at the dirt with his boot. He felt as if he was going to throw up. He didn't like being without Florida. He didn't like Sairy's question, either. "I'd still be who I am, wouldn't I? I'm without her now, aren't I? Am I different?"

Sairy studied him. "Too early to tell, I guess."

"You've been with Tiller nearly your whole life. Are you different without him?"

"I don't know," Sairy said. "Am I?"

"Too early to tell," Dallas said.

"Guess we'd better move on. You've got the compass, right? Which way now?"

"Compass?" Dallas said.

∽ 33 ∾

Z's Report

In the alley shack, Z leaned against the door. "So like I said, they've already done gone. They're outta there."

Mr. Trepid rubbed his hands rapidly back and forth as if he were warming them. "Already? Are you entirely sure? They've all gone?"

"Gone. *Zappo.*" Z picked at the wooden door frame, loosening a splinter.

Mr. Trepid paced the room, talking as he went. "Very good. Now we will start the project I mentioned. Are you prepared to keep this absolutely confidential?"

Z spat on the floor and eyed Mr. Trepid.

"Listen, if you don't trust me—"

"Oh no, no, no. Don't misunderstand me. Of course I know you'll keep this confidential. It's just that this is a most delicate—"

"I got it. Just tell me what I gotta do, and tell me what the salary will be."

"How are you at map making?" Mr. Trepid asked.

"Map making?" Z said. "That don't sound too exciting to me."

"First I want you to survey an area, and I'll tell you what to look for, and then I'll need you to make a map marking the locations of—"

"What is it exactly I'm looking for, and where am I looking?" Z picked at his teeth with the splinter.

"Down in Ruby Holler, you find their cabin, see? And then you go about, oh, let's say twenty feet out from it, in a circle, and you look for a stone, and then if you don't find it, you go, say, thirty feet out and look, and on like that until you find it," Mr. Trepid explained. He had thought about doing this himself, but he didn't like rummaging around in the woods and it would take far too much time.

"A *stone*?" Z said. "Do you have all your brains? Do you know how many stones there are in the holler? My guess is about a hundred million. Unless you are talking about a special stone, like maybe it's a green one or a red one or—"

"I don't know what it looks like, but my guess is it's not an ordinary stone. It's probably a big one, or maybe a pile of big ones."

Z raked his fingers through his matted hair. "What's so special about this stone or this pile of stones?"

Mr. Trepid had expected this question and he was prepared with an answer. "It marks a source—an oil source," he lied. "See, they were thinking of drilling up there, and I'm just a little curious as to where this oil is."

"Seems to me," Z said, "you coulda asked 'em. They probably woulda told you. If it's on their property, what do they care who knows where it is?"

"I'm not entirely sure it is on their property," Mr. Trepid said.

"So where's my salary?" Z said. "I ain't got all day."

Mr. Trepid handed him a wad of bills. "That's just a deposit. You bring me a map, with any special stones marked on it, and I'll give you the rest of the money. Don't worry, if you find the right spot, you'll get a fine salary."

"Okay, boss man, but I ain't spending a year looking. I'll go see what I see, and if it don't look too promising, I ain't gonna carry on scrabbling through the dirt."

When Mr. Trepid returned to the Boxton Creek Home, he found his wife lying on their bed with a wet cloth draped over her forehead. He knew better than to ask what was wrong, because she would tell him. She would tell him which child had broken a window and which one had broken an arm and which one had tracked in mud and which one had sassed her, and she could go on like that for hours. So instead of asking her what was wrong, he said, "I have some good news."

"I could use some good news, because that new girl broke—"

"It's very good news. How would you like to leave this place and go off to an island somewhere?"

Mrs. Trepid slipped the cloth off her head and sat up. "You have a mighty poor idea of a joke," she said.

"I'm not joking. I think in a little time, very soon maybe, we might be coming into some money."

"And where exactly is this money coming from? Is it going to drop down from heaven and land at our feet?"

"Let's just say I've got some . . . investments, some investments that should be coming through any day now."

There was a knock at their door. From outside Morgan said, "Ma'am? It's time to be getting dinner together."

Mrs. Trepid swung her legs over the side of the bed and stood up. "Lord, spare me," she said.

∞ 34 ∞

Bearings

"We'll be able to tell what direction we're going if the sun stays visible," Sairy said, "and trees will help—moss usually grows on the north side of trees, and—"

"I'm a stupid for forgetting that compass."

"You're not a stupid. I'm sure we'll be fine," Sairy said, "just fine." But she didn't sound convinced as they hacked through the brush. "Let's talk about something, Dallas. Make the time pass more easily."

"Like what?"

"Tell me about the scary toothless lunatic you and Florida keep referring to. Was he really toothless? Really a lunatic?"

"Yep."

"So tell me about him."

"Don't like to talk about it," he said.

"Sometimes talking about it is good," Sairy said. "Just pretend you're talking to Florida."

"I dunno," Dallas said.

"What was his name, and what did that toothless mouth look like?" Sairy prodded.

"Well, I guess I could talk about it a little," he said.

And so Dallas told Sairy about the toothless Mr. Dreep and his wife with the fidgety fingers, and how Mr. Dreep had locked them in the cellar and then made them spend the night there in the smelly, damp rat place.

"But that's criminal," Sairy said. "That's . . . that's . . . a terrible thing to do to anybody."

"Well, he thought I sassed him, see? He told us we were going to have to dig a well, and I told him we couldn't do that. So I guess being in the cellar was our punishment for sassing."

"Dig a well? But that's criminal. I can't get my head around this, Dallas. And even if you did sass him, that's no reason to put you in the cellar."

"That's kind of what we thought," Dallas

said, "but we weren't exactly sure."

"Not *sure*? You mean you didn't think that was strange? You didn't think it was terrible?"

Dallas shrugged. "What good would that do?"

"But . . ." Sairy looked upset and confused. "Is being in that cellar why you and Florida are so afraid of rats and mice and—"

Dallas turned away. He didn't like to dwell on these things. His mind automatically stopped the scene and played a different one. Like now: he was imagining that he was a pioneer, the first person ever to hike this hill. Maybe he'd discover something incredible up here, something no one else had ever seen.

Sairy interrupted his reverie. "How'd you get out of that toothless lunatic's place?"

"In the morning, Mr. Creep Dreep let us out and told us to follow him outside. We were so glad to be out of that rathole and breathing some real air that we followed him. Then he handed us a couple shovels and told us to start digging. We didn't want to, but he said we wouldn't get breakfast until we'd made some progress on the well. So we started digging—"

"Dallas! You were digging a well?"

"I pretended I was digging for gold—you never know, right? And Florida pretended she was digging Creep Dreep's grave, so it didn't seem so bad, the digging. We dug for about three hours, and then we saw Creep Dreep walking away from the house, like he was going out to the barn, so we watched until he was out of sight, and then we ran like nothing you've ever seen in your life. We ran and ran and ran and ran and hid in some trees, and then we heard him calling us, and he sounded really, really mad, so we stayed dead still—"

"Dallas, I just can't hardly believe this," Sairy said. "It makes me feel mighty sick to my stomach."

"It's okay," Dallas said. "Don't feel sick. We got away, didn't we? Hey, will you look at that?" They'd reached a ridge and a clearing in the trees. "Look at all those bumpy lumps of dirt. Looks like giant anthills. Not as pretty as the holler, is it?"

Sairy dabbed at her forehead. "Sure is hot. You thirsty? Got the canteen?"

"Canteen?" Dallas said.

Stiff

On the banks of the Hidden River, Tiller and Florida were finishing their lunch.

"You a little stiff?" Tiller asked, rubbing his back.

"A little," Florida said, "and I'm about swole up and itching to death from these skeeter bites."

Tiller stretched. "I didn't count on my arms being so numb. Your arms numb?"

"More sore than numb. I feel like I wrassled a hundred hogs," Florida said. "How are we going to carry on paddling with our arms all sore and pitiful?"

"We'll take it a little easier this afternoon. Let

the river carry us along. We'll be lazy paddlers."

Florida stood on the riverbank, her feet kicking at stones. "It's a stinky smell here, don't you think?" she said. "With the muddy crud and these ugly weed things."

Tiller sniffed the air. "Phew."

"It's not that pretty smell, like by the holler creek, where those itty blue flowers grow along the bank."

Tiller closed his eyes. "Oh, I know which flowers you mean."

"Tiller? You ever wish Dallas and Sairy were here with us, going on down the river?"

Tiller took a deep breath, looked down the river and up the river, and let out his breath slowly, evenly. "About every two minutes I think that," he said.

"You're not like Dallas," Florida said.

"Is that good or bad?"

"Neither one."

"Well, how am I different?" Tiller asked.

Florida kicked at the dirt. "Well, Dallas is always thinking everything will be okay and stuff, but you complain a lot—"

"Me? Complain?"

"Yeah, like I do."

"Oh," he said.

"It's just our nature." Florida knelt to examine a beetle scurrying along the bank. "I wouldn't ever want to be all by my lonesome, would you?"

Tiller felt his heart do its fluttering thing again. He couldn't imagine life without Sairy. It pained him to imagine it. And yet, not a half hour earlier, he'd been wondering what it would be like to be floating down the river by himself. *That's different,* he told himself. *That's not forever-aloneness.* He glanced at Florida and felt another flutter. He hoped Florida would never be alone.

"You hear me?" Florida said. "Would you want to be all by your lonesome?"

"No," Tiller said. "I need someone to listen to me complain."

Florida tilted a twig toward the beetle, letting it run up the side. "I didn't mean it was such a bad thing to be a complaining person," she said. "Don't go and get your feelings hurt."

As they pushed off down the river again, Tiller said, "Florida? Aside from that scary toothless lunatic's place, did you and Dallas ever get sent anywhere else?"

"Oh sure," Florida said, dipping her paddle slowly into the water. "You want to hear about the Hoppers who said we were thieves or the Cranbeps who thought we were brutes or the nasty Burgerton boys?"

"Why don't you start with the Hoppers?" he said.

36

A Long Chain

The air was hot and sticky as Sairy and Dallas thrashed their way through a thicket. Vines tangled their legs and briars jabbed their arms.

"It looked like this would be the shortest route over to that path on that hill, but I don't know now," Sairy said. "Let's stop and rest a bit, okay?" She reached into her backpack and pulled from it a yellow scarf, which she tied around her neck. If she'd worn something like that at home, Tiller would have said, *What's that around your neck? You never wear scarves.* But here, Dallas didn't know—and wouldn't care—whether she was the kind of person who would wear a yellow scarf or not. She felt a little silly thinking about it.

"There's more bugs here than in the holler, you notice that?" Dallas said, swatting at flies.

"Maybe my lucky yellow scarf will keep them away," Sairy said.

"Maybe your lucky scarf will help us find water. I bet there's a creek right down there. I bet it's real clear, not some old, muddy, poison creek, and we'll splash in it and drink as much as we want."

Sairy sat against a tree and closed her eyes. She imagined that there was an invisible ball of twine unfolding behind her, all the way back across the hills to Ruby Holler. That invisible ball of twine was right there in her hand, and she had to hold it tight, because if she let go of it, she and Dallas would be lost out here.

"What are you thinking about so serious-like?" Dallas asked her.

"Nothing much," she said.

"You're not homesick, are you?"

"Me? Shoot, no. We're on our adventure," Sairy said. "Not homesick at all."

"You know who you look like, sitting there? You know that picture in your kitchen, of the girl and the lady sitting in the woods? You look like that lady."

"I do? That's my mother, and that girl is me," Sairy said. She felt a sudden, deep longing for her dead mother, and then wondered if it was harder to miss a mother you had loved, or, like Dallas and Florida, to miss a mother you had never known.

"And that picture next to it," Dallas said, "with the two men, who are they?"

"That's Tiller and his daddy. And the one next to that, the one of the couple by the creek, that's my grandmother and grandfather. And the one next to that, that's me and Tiller and our kids."

"It's like a whole long chain of connected people," Dallas said.

"Yes," Sairy said. "I guess it is."

"Want me to build a little fire?" Dallas said. "I know it's hot, but we could eat that can of beans. They'd be better hot than cold. You got the matches?"

"Matches?" Sairy said.

37

Word Pictures

Florida and Tiller were letting the swift current carry them along. Florida had just finished telling Tiller about the Hoppers and Cranbeps and Burgertons, when Tiller made an odd sound, as if he were in pain.

"What's the matter?" she said. "You feeling poorly?" She turned around and saw him with his chin bent against his chest.

"I'm feeling like I want to strangle those Hoppers and Cranbeps and Burgerton boys," he said.

"Don't you go feeling poorly over it," she said. "You forget the worst bits after a while. Sometimes Dallas and I pretend it happened to somebody else. And you know what Dallas says?

He says that it don't mean nothing, that someday we're going to live in a glorious place, and
we'll both get married to real nice people, and
we'll each have twenty kids of our own—"

"Twenty?"

"Maybe more," Florida said, "and we won't
let anybody be mean to those kids, not ever.
And our kids will grow up and get married and
have bunches of kids of their own, and they'll
treat their kids good, and it'll go on like that
forever and ever."

Florida liked that picture. Maybe it was
good that Dallas was dreamy, she thought,
because whenever she was feeling as if everything was dark and scary and putrid, Dallas
would paint word pictures that would fly into
her mind and scatter the dark and scary things.
When they'd been locked in the toothless
lunatic's cellar, Dallas had talked all night long
about how they would live in a clean place
someday, up in the woods maybe, and all around
would be beautiful trees and clear rivers, and the
only people nearby would be good ones, nice
ones, no mean ones allowed, and on he went all
through the night, making word pictures.

∽ 38 ∽

Surveying

Z had made his way down into Ruby Holler and was sitting on Tiller and Sairy's porch. Sweat dripped from his face as he leaned back against the shaded wall.

That Trepid fellow had gone a little too far this time. Z didn't for a minute believe that Trepid wanted to know where Tiller and Sairy might have found oil. He was up to something else, and Z had a pretty good idea what it was.

Z could have refused Trepid's request right off the bat, but he figured that Trepid would just find someone else to do his dirty work, and that would not be good. At least this way, Z could stall Trepid until he figured out what to do.

Z circled the cabin, glancing in the windows.

Then he stood and looked around the yard. He
spotted a pile of stones near the well and
another pile beside the porch steps. There were
stones by the barn path and a big gray stone
near the fir tree. From his pocket, he took the
pencil and paper he'd brought with him. He
drew a square for the cabin and X's around it,
where the stones were. He hoped he found lots
of stones. Lots and lots and lots of them.

The Worrywarts

Dallas and Sairy had stopped for the day in a scrubby clearing. They were penned in by dense trees, and the ground was rocky, but it was the best place they could find to set up camp. They'd eaten cold beans and were trying to ignore their thirst.

Sairy had settled herself on a flat stone and had pulled out her block of wood and her whittling knife, when Dallas said, "Sairy? I don't get it. I mean, that you'd want to go someplace else where you don't have your own bed that you're used to, and you don't have all that good food you make, and there are all these bugs and—"

Sairy sniffed. "Well, if we ever do go to Kangadoon, I am sure it will be worth the trip."

"*If* we go to Kangadoon?" Dallas said. *"If?"*

"I meant *when* we go," Sairy said. "I don't know why I said *if.*"

Dallas stared at Sairy, who looked as if she might cry, and that shocked him. He couldn't imagine her crying, but trying to picture it made him remember a time when Mrs. Trepid had grabbed ahold of Florida and shook her. "Why don't you ever cry?" Mrs. Trepid had demanded, and Florida had replied, "'Cause I don't putrid want to."

But Florida did cry sometimes. She'd cried at the Hoppers' and the Cranbeps' and the Burgertons' and at the Creepy Dreeps'. Dallas hadn't cried at those places. He didn't know why he hadn't. Maybe it was because Florida was crying enough for the two of them, or because he'd wanted to cheer her up.

Dallas had cried after Joey died, but no one saw him cry except Florida. And sometimes at night at the Home he cried, and if Florida heard him, she would sneak into the closet and lift the cardboard flap and say, "Don't think about it, Dallas. It will go away."

Out in the woods now with Sairy, Dallas pulled out his own block of wood and studied it. He'd already chipped at one end, but he hadn't figured out what was inside yet. "What's that one you're carving?" he asked Sairy.

"Not sure yet," Sairy said. "Just have to see what comes out. How about yours?"

"No idea. Maybe another robin."

"You don't have to find a bird in yours," Sairy said. "Maybe there's something else inside yours."

"Like what?" Dallas said.

"I don't know, could be anything at all."

"It's probably a slug," Dallas said. "Or a slimy worm." He felt odd, as if he was talking like Florida. "Or a putrid rat thing." It made him laugh, to talk like Florida.

"You know what I was just thinking?" Sairy said. "I was remembering a time when Tiller and I were out walking in the holler—this was a long time ago, before our kids were even born— and there, in the middle of the path, was a perfect piece of wood, and we both reached for it."

"Did you fight over it?" Dallas asked. "You pull it back and forth?"

"Not exactly, I mean not the way you're thinking. We stayed there a few minutes, bent over, both of us touching that wood, and I was thinking, *Why doesn't he let go and let me have it? If he loves me, he'll let me have it.* Tiller was probably thinking the same thing: *If she loves me, she'll let me have it.*" Sairy put one finger against her lips and tapped softly, as if she were coaxing more words out of her mouth. "Finally, I said that I thought there was a perfect bird in that piece of wood. I could see it in my mind, this little bird nestled in that wood, waiting for me to set it free."

Dallas examined the piece of wood in his hands, wondering why he couldn't see what was inside.

"And," Sairy continued, "Tiller said that he could see a perfect *boat* in that piece of wood, a perfect, perfect boat just waiting to be let loose."

"So which was it, a boat or a bird? Who won?"

Sairy tapped at her lips. "He gave in first. He

said, 'You have it,' and I snatched it up and was so happy, and on we walked, and as we walked, I started to feel bad. I was trying to picture myself taking the first slivers off this perfect piece of wood. What if I ruined it? What if there was no perfect bird inside? So I told Tiller, 'Here, you have it.'"

"Did he take it?" Dallas asked.

"He took it so fast, I didn't even have time to blink," Sairy said.

"And he made a perfect boat out of that piece of wood?"

"No. For days and days I saw him holding that piece of wood, turning it around and around. He'd get out his knife, but he just couldn't seem to take the first cut. Then you know what he did? He placed that piece of wood on our dresser, and he said, 'Sairy, I'm putting this here for a while. It'll belong to both of us. Whoever wants to get started on it can do it.'"

"So you grabbed it, right?"

"I wanted to," Sairy said. "I could hardly contain myself. I'd go in the bedroom and touch that piece of wood, but I just could not put my knife to it. And then when I wasn't in there, I'd be worrying that *he* was in there getting started on it."

"You two sure are weird," Dallas said.

"Everybody's a little weird, Dallas."

"So who finally got the wood?"

Sairy grinned. "It's still there, right on our dresser, a piece of wood with who-knows-what inside."

Dallas held his block of wood to his ear, as if maybe he could hear what was inside. "Sairy? Are we lost?"

"Lost? Us? Shoot, we're on this scrubby patch of dirt on this hillside. Maybe we don't know where exactly this hillside is, but I'm sure we'll be fine, just fine." She reached up to touch her yellow scarf, as if it might bring them luck.

"Sairy, did you ever wonder if Tiller might get used to being on his own?"

Sairy flashed him a worried look. "I was thinking about that a little earlier," Sairy said. "You can read my mind. I was thinking how maybe we'd get used to this hiking, and maybe

I'd stop thinking about the holler or Tiller, and then I felt bad, like what if Tiller forgot to think about me?"

"Yeah," Dallas said, "and what if Florida gets used to traveling on the river and doesn't want to come back and maybe she won't want me tagging along?"

"Listen to us," Sairy said. "A couple of worry-warts."

"Yeah," Dallas said. "A couple of stupid worrywarts."

∽ 40 ∽

Babies in the Box

Tiller and Florida had traveled the length of Hidden River and had spent the last two hours portaging into the Goochee River.

"It's so beastly hot," Florida said. "And I thought you said portaging would be easy. It wasn't easy. Look how long it took us, lugging all our stuff out of the boat and up the bank and over those rocks and then dragging that heavy boat up the bank and—"

"Why'd we bring so much stuff?" Tiller grumbled. "Every time we portage, we're going to have to lug all this crud." He eyed the dark storm clouds in the distance. "We'd better get that tent up or we're going to get soaked tonight," Tiller said. "Smell that? It's a real goose-drownder that's coming our way."

Later, as the storm clouds broke above them, they sat under the canopy of the tent while the remains of their fire steamed and fizzled. Tiller was carving a fishing boat, and Florida was staring at her piece of wood.

"Look what a mess I've made of this," she said. "I don't know what the cruddy crud it is."

"You don't have to know when you start out," Tiller said. "Just see what comes out. Sometimes you have to sneak up on it. Pretend you're just moving your hand, your knife, and you don't think you're making anything. Then all of a sudden you look down, quick, and sometimes you can tell right then. But still you pretend you don't know because you don't want what's inside to curl up tighter and refuse to come out. You want to be gentle with it."

Florida closed her eyes, rolled the wood around in her hands, and then she opened her eyes quickly and stared down at the wood. Nothing. "Whoa!" she said. "Did you see that lightning? Are we supposed to be out here when that stuff is crashing around us? What if it hits a tree and the tree falls on us and konks us dead?"

"I guess someone will find our smashed-up bodies someday," Tiller said.

"Tiller? You ever seen a dead person? I mean a real dead person, not a picture of one."

Tiller thought about his father, lying cold on his bed, and his mother in her coffin. He thought about his two best friends who'd died last year. "Yes," he said. "I've seen a few. Have you ever seen a dead person?"

"Yep."

"And who was that?"

"A boy in our orphanage place. Dallas couldn't save him."

"What?"

So she told him about Joey and his fever and about Dallas watching over him and Joey saying, "Who am I? Who am I?" and Dallas trying to get him to breathe again.

"That's terrible," Tiller said. "Where were the Trepids?"

"They were there. Mr. Trepid was crying, and Mrs. Trepid was yelling at him, and—"

"Terrible, terrible."

"You know what? Dallas didn't talk—I mean he didn't say a single word—for a whole month after that."

"What about you? How did you feel?"

"I felt like it was probably going to be me who died next," Florida said, "and so I wrote my name on my arm in red ink so even if I was delirious with a fever, I'd know who I was, and I told Dallas that even if he couldn't get me to breathe again, it wouldn't be his fault. If I didn't breathe again, it would probably be because I didn't have any room left for air."

Tiller poked at the damp wood and ashes. "Florida? You mind if I ask you something? If it's nosy, you just ignore it."

"Like what?"

"I was thinking about your name. *Florida*. It's a mighty nice name. You probably don't have any idea how you got it, do you?"

"I only know what those putrid Trepids told us."

"And what was that?" Tiller asked.

"They told us we were in a box on their porch, little babies, both of us in the same box, and there wasn't any note or anything. We were wrapped up in a clean white blanket, and the box was lined with papers, well, not papers exactly, but pamphlets, you know those kind you see for people going on trips and stuff?"

"What, like tourist pamphlets, that sort of thing?"

"That's right," Florida said. "And I was lying on one that said *Fly to Florida!* and Dallas was lying on one that said *Destination: Dallas!* and so they gave us those names. I was the Florida baby and Dallas was the Dallas baby."

"I wonder why those things were in the bottom of that box," Tiller said. "You ever wonder that?"

"You know what? I never did wonder that, not until you just said it. Our mother probably just found an old box and it had that stuff in it and she didn't pay it any attention. She probably just wrapped us up in that clean white blanket and put us inside. Maybe she wrote a note about how awful she felt having to give us up, and on that note was our real names, but maybe the wind blew that note away. You think?"

"Could be," Tiller said. "How about your last name? Carter, is it? How'd you get that?"

"On the side of the box, it said *Carter's Produce.*"

"Ah," Tiller said. "Well, Florida Carter is a lot better than Florida Produce."

"Or Florida Box."

Tiller touched the piece of wood Florida had been whittling away at. "You see what's happening there? You've been talking and carving and paying it no attention and now, look there . . ."

Florida stared down at it. "What do you think that is? Some curly-headed thing?"

"I don't know, but I bet if you keep paying it no attention, it'll come out."

"That's just what I'm going to do," Florida said. "Pay it no attention whatsoever."

41

Shopping

When Mrs. Trepid entered Burley's Department Store and felt the cool air swirl around her, she put her hand against the damp hair on her neck. *Such a relief to be where it is cool,* she thought. *Such a relief to be where it is quiet.*

In the dress department, she wandered from rack to rack, occasionally pulling out a dress and holding it against her. *Too dowdy,* she thought, or *too prissy.* And then she saw it: the perfect dress. It was pale blue silk with tiny pink flowers, ankle length and sleeveless, with a low, scooped neck. She held it against her and swished the bottom across her legs.

Mrs. Trepid carried it to the fitting room, and once she had the dress on and zipped, she turned to look in the mirror. *This is how I should always look,* she thought. She stepped out into the hallway where there was a larger mirror, and she turned this way and that.

A young salesgirl walked by with an armload of clothes. "That dress was made for you," the girl said to Mrs. Trepid.

"Do you really think so?" Mrs. Trepid said, turning a full revolution so that the girl could see it from all angles.

"Oh yes," the girl said. "And you could wear it for so many occasions."

Mrs. Trepid put her fingertips to her chin and regarded her reflection. "You know, I think you may be right."

In the dressing room, Mrs. Trepid changed back into her own dress, took out her glasses, and examined the price tag. *My goodness,* she thought. *That much money for a skimpy little dress?* She thought about what her husband had said about his investments and about moving to an island. *This would be perfect for an evening on an island.*

She found the salesgirl at the counter. "You know," she said to the girl, "I can't quite make up my mind about this dress."

"But it's made for you," the girl said. "You know what you could do? You could put it on layaway. Pay a little now and a little each month, and then it seems like you get it for practically nothing. I do it all the time."

Mrs. Trepid felt embarrassed that the girl could sense that she couldn't afford the dress. "Of course I don't really need to use layaway," Mrs. Trepid said. "I could buy it right now if I wanted."

"Oh," the girl said.

"But I might just try that layaway. Why not?"

After she left the dress department, Mrs. Trepid wandered around the store, touching purses and scarves and slips. She sauntered back through the dress department, pausing at the rack where she'd found her dress. As she did so, she heard the salesgirl talking to another customer.

"That dress was made for you," the girl said to the customer.

Mrs. Trepid felt foolish, and hurriedly left the

department. But as she stepped out onto the hot sidewalk, she thought about her blue silk dress with the pink flowers. She saw herself on an island, sitting by the ocean, sipping a cool drink.

On the outskirts of Prosper City, some fifty miles from Boxton, Mr. Trepid found a Cadillac showroom. Inside, he circled the three cars on display, casually examining the tags which listed the specifications and equipment, as well as the price, of each vehicle. After he examined all three, he returned to the red convertible and stood with his hand on the driver's door. He could smell the leather interior.

"May I help you?" came a voice from behind him.

Mr. Trepid kept his hand on the door as he turned to greet the salesman. The man was taller than Mr. Trepid and smiled down on him.

"I'm considering buying a new car," Mr. Trepid said soberly. "Perhaps one like this." He tapped the door of the red convertible.

"What are you driving now?" the salesman asked.

"What, now? Me? I'm driving a Porsche," he lied.

The salesman glanced out the window, as if looking for Mr. Trepid's Porsche.

"It's in the shop right now," Mr. Trepid said. "That's why I'm looking for a new car. Getting tired of that Porsche!" He tried to look disgusted at the thought of his Porsche in the shop. What Mr. Trepid really owned was a ten-year-old Plymouth. He'd had the foresight to park it three blocks away so that the salesmen wouldn't see his battered old car.

"So you'll be doing a trade-in then?" the salesman asked. "On your Porsche?"

"Probably not," Mr. Trepid said, smiling heartily at the salesman. "Think I'll give the Porsche to the wife."

"Ah," the salesman said. "Will you be wanting financing? Would you like to talk with our finance manager?"

Mr. Trepid tapped the door once more. "I may pay cash," he said.

"I see. What did you say your name was, sir?"

"Trepid. George Trepid."

"Well, Mr. Trepid, are there any questions I can answer for you, sir?"

Mr. Trepid had a hundred questions, but he wasn't going to ask them of this salesman. He didn't want to appear ignorant. "I think not," Mr. Trepid said coolly. "I'm going to check out another dealership first."

"I think you'll find we can give you the best deal," the salesman said. "Here's my card. Anything I can do for you, you just let me know."

"Thank you," Mr. Trepid said, stuffing the card in his shirt pocket and glancing at his watch. "And now I must be off. Perhaps I'll see you again." He hurried to the door and stepped out into the bright sunlight. *Well!* he thought. *I think that went very well indeed.*

42

Dorkhead

In the morning, as Sairy was repacking, she lifted her half-carved piece and said, "You know what I do with these carvings sometimes? I make up names for them. Silly names, like Peeker and Bitty Beak, just made-up names."

"I have a made-up name," Dallas said.

"What do you mean?"

"You know, *Dallas*. It's just a name those Trepids got from a box."

"A box?"

And so he told her about the box that he and Florida had been found in, and when he finished, Sairy said, "Dallas, remember when we got your passport?"

"Stupid picture. I look like a dorkhead."

"No, you don't. You look mighty handsome. But did you notice the birth date on it?"

"Yeah, March third. Dorkheads. My birthday's July twenty-ninth."

"But maybe . . . maybe your birthday really is March third."

"Naw," Dallas said. "You think? Naw. I don't want a March birthday."

"You're right. I understand. That Trepid fellow probably just made a mistake."

But later, as they set off down the hill, Dallas remembered, or thought he remembered, the Trepids' telling him that since they didn't have any idea of when Florida or Dallas were really born, the Trepids had listed their birth date as the day they arrived at the orphanage. So, Dallas thought, their real birthday must have been several months before that. Maybe March third *was* his real birthday. It made him mad. A person ought to know when his birthday was.

43

Loops

When they'd first set off down the river, Florida had imagined that all of the rivers they would travel would be as narrow as the one passing through Ruby Holler, and that it was all just water, running smoothly on and on and on. What she now knew, after only a day and a half on the river, was that rivers were like living things, and they had many faces. You might come around a bend and *wham!* The river suddenly widened out and ran faster. And just when you'd get used to that wide rushing river, you'd go around another bend and *wham!* It narrowed again and put a few rocks in your way and a few eddies to swirl you around and then maybe a sandbar to stop you short.

You might start out in the morning with the river like a velvety shimmery cloth, and by noon it could be full of ripples and waves and splashes. You could watch both wind and rain coming at you from the distance, marking the water. And as the sun went down, all sorts of golden light flashed here and there, and long shadows stretched farther and farther, until it was all one big black shadowy thing out there.

As they paddled along on this new morning, Florida said, "Tonight, I'm going to catch another big fish, like last night. Wasn't that a beauty? Didn't that taste like the best thing you ever tasted in your life? I am a natural-born fisherwoman! Maybe my mother was a fisherwoman. You think?"

"Could be," Tiller said.

"Your arm okay from where I hooked you?"

"Uh-huh," he said.

"You think we can get that reel untangled?"

"Uh-huh."

"Tiller? How come you don't get mad at me

when I goof up?" She heard his paddle dip in and out of the water, in and out. "You hear me?"

"I heard you. Maybe I'm too old to get mad, or maybe what *you* consider goofs aren't what *I* consider goofs—it's just stuff that happens."

"Most people would consider everything I do a goof."

"Then they're just putrid," Tiller said, and he laughed. "*Putrid*—what a great word."

"So you don't mind too much about me and Dallas being in Ruby Holler?" She heard Tiller's paddle dipping in and out of the water, in and out. "If you do mind, you can say so." She stared at the river ahead. Why didn't he answer her? What was he thinking?

Finally he said, "Florida, it's been putrid having you and Dallas in Ruby Holler."

"What?" She snapped her head around.

"I was just kidding," he said. "It's been real interesting having you and Dallas in Ruby Holler."

"Good interesting or bad interesting?" she asked.

"You know I can't say bad interesting, or

you'd probably tip me out of this boat, so I guess I'll have to say good interesting."

Florida stared at the water. "Tiller? How come we're paddling so hard and getting no-where? Does it feel like we're going upstream instead of downstream?"

"You know when we went to the right of that island back there?" Tiller said. "And then the river looped?"

"Yeah, I remember. It's been looping ever since."

"Maybe we should have gone the other way—to the other side of that island," Tiller said.

"What does the map say?"

Tiller placed his paddle across his knees and reached for the map. "Don't see any island on this map. Don't see any loops."

"You're not telling me we're lost, are you?"

"I think we might be a little bit lost," Tiller said.

"If it's just a little bit lost, that's okay, I guess."

∾ 44 ∾

Progress

Z was in his usual place leaning against the door as Mr. Trepid paced around the shack, anxious to hear about Z's progress.

"And you say you've spotted some possible sites?" Trepid said. "Very good. Approximately how many?"

"So far, about twenty-five," Z said.

Trepid halted. *"Twenty-five?"* he sputtered. "That's . . . that's . . . too many."

"Like I said before, there's a lot of stones in that holler," Z said.

"But *twenty-five*? Are you looking for big stones or unusual piles of stones, or are you marking any old stone you see?"

Z pulled a stick of gum from his pocket, unwrapped it, and popped it in his mouth. "If I marked any old stone I saw, I'd have marked about two thousand by now."

"Have you finished surveying?" Trepid asked.

"Nope. Need a little more time."

"When are they returning?"

"Not really sure when they'll be back," Z said. "I'll have to check into that."

"You do that," Trepid said, "and speed it up. And go back over those stones you've marked and be sure they all look . . . promising. We'll meet again tomorrow, same time."

Z chewed his gum and waited.

Trepid said, "Okay, okay. Here's a little more salary. That ought to cover another day's work. The rest will come if this produces any results." He handed Z some bills and reached behind him for the door handle.

Z didn't budge. His gaze was fixed on Trepid's gold front tooth.

"Meeting's over," Trepid said.

∞ 45 ∞

The Rock

It had been raining hard all afternoon, and the river was rushing along.

"Whew!" Florida called over the noise of the surging water. "We are really zipping—we must be going downstream now." The water splashed over the bow, soaking her legs. "We might be drenched and lost and heading for the worst rapids you ever saw, but at least we're going in the right direction, don't you think, Tiller?" She swiveled to look at Tiller, whose face and poncho were soaked.

"What's a little rain?" he said. "What's a little water? What's a little lostness?" He dipped his paddle hard into the water.

"Charge!" Florida yelled above the noise of the river. Ahead was a bend, and they aimed for the middle of it.

The wind and rain whipped against her face, and she loved the feel of it, all of it: the charging down the river, the paddle diving in and out, the water spraying up over the bow, the rain pelting down on her. Around the bend they flew, and there, directly in front of them, was a huge boulder. "Tiller," she called. "Rock. Turn!"

The boat veered sharply to the right of the boulder and caught in a swirl of water, plunging them back toward the boulder. The boat smacked against it, once, twice, hard, and the water swirled against the back of the boat, spinning it and then, in one mighty surge, tipping it.

When Florida surfaced, she was already far downstream of the boulder, spluttering and coughing. Looking behind her, she had a quick glimpse of her life jacket bobbing way back there, and then she was under again.

This is it, she thought. *I am going to die.*

When she resurfaced, she glimpsed Tiller upstream, trying to cling to one end of the boat.

"Grab on to something, anything!" he yelled.

"I can't swim!"

She saw the boat reel and smash hard against another rock. Just before she was pulled under again, she saw Tiller lose his grip and disappear beneath the boat.

How can water push so hard? she thought. *Help me, Dallas, help me, help me, help me.*

46

Stones in the Holler

It was a glorious morning in the holler. A cool front had come through during the night, and the air was fresh and clear, with a mild breeze sifting through the treetops, ruffling leaves.

Z was ambling along, poking a stick at various stones. He bent down to gather three stones and pile them near a tree trunk. *There,* he thought, *that looks about right.* Earlier, he'd collected flat stones from the creek and piled them carefully near a birch grove. With a piece of charred wood he'd brought with him, he made mysterious-looking squiggles on the top stone. *Perfect.*

He pulled out a fresh piece of paper and started a new map. The cabin was in the center. He marked the two new piles he'd made, and then he walked around the cabin, about twenty feet out from it, marking large stones that had already been there, and new piles of stones that he'd gathered.

Next he walked up the opposite hill and looked around. He spotted a faint path winding past a clump of violets and curving beyond a funny-looking bush. He followed the path in and out of the trees until it seemed to end beneath an overhanging willow. Near the base of the willow was a smooth gray stone, half covered with leaves. He bent down and lifted the stone, discovering freshly turned earth beneath it. He dug only a few inches before hitting something hard and metallic.

Z scraped the dirt from the top of a metal box. On it was painted *Sairy's! Keep Out!* The latch was locked. Z stuffed Sairy's box in his sack and set off in search of a *Tiller* box.

Running

D allas and Sairy had reached a summit and could see a narrow path spiraling steeply downward toward a stream.

"Water!" Dallas shouted. "Real water! We may be completely lost, but there's water!" Dallas picked up a stick from the path and tapped it in front of him. "Hey, Sairy," he called behind him. "I'll meet you farther down," and with that, he took off running.

He sailed down the path, dodging roots, whooping and laughing. As he rounded a bend, a small furry animal leaped in front of him. It looked like a rat. Dallas jumped over it, skidded, and landed hard on his back. Something crumpled inside him. *Florida,* he thought. *Florida's in trouble.*

More Shopping

Mrs. Trepid had taken the bus to Prosper City and was standing in front of the First Avenue Jewelry store. She wasn't sure what had brought her to this place, only that she was here and wanted very much to go inside.

She took a deep breath, straightened her back, and opened the door. Overhead, slender tubes of light beamed down on the display cases. The counters were polished to a high sheen, and inside the display cases, shiny bright mirrors reflected gold and silver and sparkly gems.

A man in a dark suit drifted toward her. "May I help you?" he asked. "Are you looking for something in particular?"

Mrs. Trepid glanced at the display case, spotting a gold necklace with tiny red and white stones in it. "That's nice," she said, indicating the necklace.

The man slipped his hand into his pocket, removed a ring of keys, and deftly unlocked the case, sliding out a mirrored base on which the necklace rested. "A lovely choice," he said, releasing it from the base. He tilted the counter's mirror toward her as she tried it on. "Ah," he said. "Absolutely perfect. It's *you*."

Mrs. Trepid smiled at her reflection. The necklace *was* perfect.

"Rubies and opals, of course," the man said. "And the finest gold, of course."

"Of course," Mrs. Trepid murmured. *Rubies and opals?* she thought. *Real rubies? Real opals?*

"Is it for a special occasion?" the man asked.

"What? Oh, yes. Yes, it is." Her mind raced. *What sort of special occasion?* "A cruise, actually," she blurted. "My husband and I are going on a special cruise. To an island."

"In the Caribbean?" the man said.

"Why, yes," Mrs. Trepid lied. "How did you know?"

"That's where a beautiful woman like yourself *should* be going."

Mrs. Trepid's face reddened. "Why, thank you."

"Does Madam wish to know the price?" The man smiled, a gentle, kind smile.

Mrs. Trepid nodded.

"Eighteen thousand dollars," he said. "Completely reasonable, of course, for such a fine work of art."

"Oh, completely," Mrs. Trepid said, brushing at a piece of lint on her sleeve. She thought surely she had heard wrong. *Eighteen thousand dollars for a necklace?* Mrs. Trepid felt warm and agitated. "Is your air conditioning working?"

The man hurried to the thermostat. "Yes, it seems to be working. Is Madam not comfortable?"

She fidgeted with the necklace's clasp. "Like you say, it's perfect, and rubies and opals are . . . so . . ." She didn't know how to finish. She pretended to study the gems. "I'm just not sure this will go with my gown." *Gown? Why did I say "gown"? What a silly word,* gown.

"Madam is more than welcome to bring her gown in and try it on with the necklace," the man said. He followed her to the door and opened it for her. "Shall I put the necklace aside for you?"

Mrs. Trepid hurried through the door. She wanted to say, *No, no, lock it up, take it away.* Instead she said, "Sure."

"Your name?"

"Trepid," she said. "Marjorie Trepid. Bye-bye," and she rushed down the street wondering why she had given her real name and why she had added that silly *bye-bye.*

She didn't stop until she was several blocks beyond the jeweler's. When she did stop, she leaned against a building. *Eighteen thousand dollars.* She could hardly imagine that kind of money. *Where did people make that kind of money, that they could throw it away on eighteen-thousand-dollar necklaces?* Her mind reeled with all the other things that could be done with that much money.

The following day, Mr. Trepid made his way to the same jewelry store, carefully removing his watch before he entered. He scuttled quickly to the watch counter and peered inside.

"May I help you?" the salesman asked.

Mr. Trepid had decided to be firm and decisive. "I'm looking for a watch. There—something like that." He pointed to the display case.

"A perfect choice," the man said, removing it from the case. "Would the gentleman care to try it?"

"Yes," Mr. Trepid said, offering his wrist.

"One of our finest," the salesman said. "Have you owned one of these before?"

"Yes, yes, I have," Mr. Trepid lied. "Lost it, unfortunately."

"Lost? What a tragedy."

Mr. Trepid tried to look forlorn. "Absolutely," he said. "One doesn't like to lose such a fine watch."

"No, sir, one does not."

Mr. Trepid turned his wrist this way and that.

"Perfect," the salesman said. "It's made for you."

Yes, Mr. Trepid thought. *It does look as if it were made especially for me.*

The salesman was saying something about

the quality of the gold and diamonds, and then, "Does the gentleman wish to know the price?"

"The price? Why not?"

"Nine thousand dollars," the salesman said. "Quite reasonable, of course, given the diamonds and—"

"Absolutely reasonable," Mr. Trepid interrupted.

"Does the gentleman wish to purchase now?"

Mr. Trepid's eyes roamed the display case. "You know," he said quickly, "there are a few others there I would like to try also."

The salesman glanced down at the case.

"But I'm in too much of a hurry right now," Mr. Trepid said. "Perhaps I should come back when I have more time." He pulled at the strap, releasing it. As he placed the watch back on the counter, his fingers trembled. "Yes, quite a hurry today." He turned toward the door. "I will be back though, yes, I will."

"Would you like me to place it aside for you?"

"Absolutely," Mr. Trepid said, reaching for the door handle.

"Your name, sir?"

"Trepid. George Trepid." Mr. Trepid could not wait to get out of the store.

"Trepid?" the salesman said. "Ah, Trepid. You're going on a cruise?"

But Mr. Trepid didn't hear him because he was already on the sidewalk, lunging down the street. *Nine thousand dollars for a watch?* he thought. *What a rip-off.*

But as he scurried down the walk, Mr. Trepid glanced at his wrist. *It did look spectacular on me,* he thought. *Perhaps the quality of the diamonds, yes, it was the diamonds. Maybe nine thousand dollars is quite reasonable for a watch with real diamonds.*

∾ 49 ∾

Underwater

The boat was upside down, and Tiller was beneath it, trying to cling to one of the struts as the boat hurtled through the water. He was dragged along, smashed against rocks, dunked under surges of water. Each time he tried to get out from underneath the boat, it slammed down on him.

He was desperately hoping Florida had made it to shore, and he was regretting that neither he nor Florida had been wearing their life jackets. *Stupid old man,* he thought. As if the river agreed with him, it surged over him, dunking him and loosening his grasp on the boat. He felt it fly free as he tumbled along underwater.

Florida can't swim. If only he'd known that beforehand. He felt suddenly weak and powerless, as limp as a rag doll.

Downriver, Florida was clinging to a boulder in the middle of the river. It was slimy and mossy; her hands were slipping. She remembered a boy at the Home telling her about learning to float. He said, "You take in a huge bunch of air and lie there like a dead man."

As the raging water loosened her grip on the boulder, she gulped in air and closed her eyes. *I am going to float like a dead man,* she thought. *I hope I don't end up a dead girl.*

For a few seconds, she felt her body suspended on the water, and then she was slammed against a floating log and knocked under the water. Her knees scraped rocks on the bottom. *Maybe it's not so deep here. If only I could stand. If only this putrid water would quit pushing me.*

The Feeling

D allas was lying on the path, feeling like a scarecrow whose stuffing had been pulled out.

"You okay?" Sairy said, running up behind him.

"Slipped," he said. His head throbbed, and his arm felt as if the Burgerton boys had been at work on him. He closed his eyes, and as he did so, he saw an image of Joey, only this time Joey was trying to breathe air into Dallas. "Sairy," he said, "I just want you to know that if I die, it's not your fault."

"What?" she said. "Die? Do you feel like you're going to *die*?"

"No, but I'm just saying—"

"Hush," she said, reaching for her backpack. "I'm hoping I brought enough money in case we need to get you to a doctor. Don't suppose there are any understone funds out here, hmm?"

Understone funds? What was it about the understone funds that had been nagging at the back of Dallas's brain? Something was bothering him; he couldn't figure out what it was.

"I hope we're not too awful far from Ruby Holler or Boxton," Sairy said.

Boxton. The Trepids. Understone funds. Uh-oh.

"You okay?" Sairy said. "You a little dizzy?"

Dallas was trying to remember when he and Florida had run into Mr. Trepid outside Grace's Diner. Had they mentioned the understone funds? Why had they done that?

"Dallas?"

A little movie was playing in Dallas's head. In it, he saw Mr. Trepid roaming through the holler, searching for the understone funds.

"Sairy?" he said. "I did a stupid, stupid thing."

"Nonsense," she said. "Anyone can fall. It's not your fault you fell."

Dallas closed his eyes again. He was going

to have to tell her. And then, suddenly washing over him was that feeling, again, that Florida was in trouble. "Sairy! Wait. Something's wrong with Florida—"

"Florida? What are you talking about?"

"I know it. I feel it. Something's wrong. Something's happened. We've got to go find her and Tiller." He scrambled to his feet. "We've *got* to. Something's awful wrong." His chest felt so tight that he had to gulp for air.

Sairy put her hand to her throat and said, "Maybe it's Tiller, not Florida. I've got this feeling—"

"Well, so do I," Dallas said, "so let's get moving."

They scrambled down the path to the stream at its bottom, frantically trying to get their bearings, but they had no idea which direction to turn.

"Just take a wild stab," Sairy said. "Upstream or downstream? What does your gut tell you?"

"Downstream," Dallas said.

They headed off along the bank, clambering over roots and rocks, weaving through thickets. From the distance came the crack of a gun, followed by a shout. On the opposite side of the stream, two young men emerged. They were scruffy, maybe sixteen or seventeen years old, and both carried guns.

The taller of the two young men said to the other, "Heck, we almost bagged us a couple of people with that shot." To Sairy and Dallas, he said, "You seen a deer come through here?"

"No," Sairy said.

The shorter boy said, "I told you it warn't no deer. It was a bobcat."

"I ought to be able to tell a bobcat from a deer," the taller boy said. "What're you two doing up here?"

"Hiking," Sairy said. "Don't suppose you can tell us where we are?"

The taller boy took a swig from a hip flask and wiped his mouth on his sleeve. "You don't know where you are?"

"Not precisely," Sairy said. "We started out in Ruby Holler and that's where we're aiming to get back to."

"Ruby Holler?" the shorter boy said. "Never heard of it."

"How about Boxton?" Dallas said. "You know where that is?"

"Sure," the taller boy said, and he was about to say more when the other boy interrupted him.

"You do not," he said. "You've never been to Boxton. You don't know where it is, see?"

"Oh. Must've been thinking of some other town."

"Well, do you know where we could find a phone?" Sairy said.

"Sure," the shorter boy said. "Sure. You just keep on going downstream, and real close by, there's a little diner, see? You can get something to eat and use the phone. Tell you what. We'll even watch your stuff for you, if you want. We'll wait here for you. That stuff looks pretty heavy."

"That's mighty nice of you," Sairy said. "You say it's real close, this diner?"

"Sure, five minutes away."

Sairy removed her backpack and set it on the ground. "Okay, then. Dallas, you ready?"

Dallas was torn. His old self would have

leaped at the chance to dump his heavy backpack and go get food, but what he was hearing
in his head was Florida saying, *Don't trust 'em!*

"Dallas?" Sairy repeated. "Come on, let's go
to that diner and find out where we are. We can
use the phone and get a message to Z—"

"Z? Is that the guy who hauled the boat to
the river?"

"Yes," Sairy said. "He'll know how to find
Tiller and Florida—and us."

As Sairy and Dallas started toward the diner,
Dallas glanced back at the boys, who were now
sitting beside Sairy's and Dallas's backpacks,
smiling.

"Bye-bye," they called. "We'll be right here,
waiting for you."

Z

As Z drove down the road away from Ruby Holler, he wished he'd never gotten mixed up with Trepid, and he hoped he could keep Trepid at bay until Tiller and Sairy got back.

What Trepid hadn't reckoned on was that Z had known Tiller and Sairy most of his life, and that Z's cabin was over the far side of the holler, which made Z their nearest neighbor. It was Z who had driven Tiller and Florida and the boat down to the river, and Sairy and Dallas back home again. It was Z they had asked to keep an eye on their place while they were gone, and it was Z who would meet Tiller and

Florida at the end of their journey and drive
them and the boat home.

Z glanced at himself in his rearview mirror.
I gotta get a haircut, he thought. *And a shave. And
clean up my place. Maybe wash these clothes. Maybe
clean up this here truck, too.*

He wished Sairy and Tiller would hurry
up and get back. He needed to tell them about
Trepid, and he also needed to make his con-
fessions.

His first confession would be easy enough.
He'd tell them that he was the one who'd gotten Dallas's passport. He hadn't seen any harm
in doing that job for Trepid, except that he
couldn't locate a birth certificate so he'd had a
friend forge one. Z hadn't felt too guilty about
that until he'd discovered that Dallas was the
boy who was going to accompany Sairy on her
trip. He'd have to tell Sairy the truth.

His second confession was going to be
harder.

He thought about Tiller and Sairy's place,
with its cozy quilts and always the smell of
something good cooking. *I'm a lousy cook.
There's fleas in my place.*

Z opened the glove compartment and fished through the mess of papers inside. He pulled out one wrinkled piece and smoothed it against the steering wheel. It was a copy of the hospital records he'd found after Sairy, Dallas, Tiller, and Florida had gone off on their trips.

He didn't know what had made him go back and look at more records. He didn't need to; he'd already gotten a passport for Dallas. But he'd found it interesting, looking at those things, at the lists of all the babies born and how much they weighed and how long they were. One little baby weighed only four ounces. *That's not much more than a little bird,* he thought.

Z had already checked the records for February and March of the year Dallas and Florida were born. Now he flipped to April. And there, in the entry for April fourth, it listed twins born at seven forty-five A.M. A boy and a girl. His eye moved to the middle column, where the mother's name was listed.

He thought he was going to have a heart attack.

That's my wife. My old wife. My only old wife.

He tried to do some quick figuring, but his

mind was racing. He could hardly breathe. *Was that the year she left?* She'd left one snowy cold November day. A snowy, snowy, freezing, cold November day. *What year was that?*

An idea took hold in his brain and raced around like a rabid dog. *Those twins could be my twins. They could be my kids. I could be a father.*

Z didn't know what to do with this information. *It's too much for a man to take in. I gotta let my head find a place to put it.*

Maybe he should tell those kids straight out and take them to his place, and they'd be a ready-made family. But he didn't know the first thing about kids. Maybe he'd better study up first. Maybe he'd better check what year his wife left.

Now as he drove away from the holler, he folded the paper and shoved it back in the glove compartment. *Maybe oughta learn how to cook first. Maybe oughta save up some money. Maybe oughta . . .*

And on he went down the road, thinking *Maybe oughta, maybe oughta. . . .*

The One-Log Raft

Florida tumbled along underwater, knees and elbows scraping rocks. The current surged and rolled over her, batting her around like an old sack. When she could push against the bottom hard enough, she lunged to the surface to gulp air before the river dunked her again. She was mad: mad at the river, at the rocks, and at herself for not knowing how to swim. *You are not going to beat me, putrid river!*

Her next lunge to the surface brought her forehead smack against a wide log, floating free in the water. She grabbed for it, pulling herself across it, hanging on as it careened wildly down the river. *A raft*, she thought. *A crazy, one-log raft!*

She had no control over the log, but it kept her head above water so that she could breathe more than one gulp at a time. Ahead the river churned toward the next bend. *If only I could get to the bank,* she thought. *If only I could see Tiller.* It was hard to look back without tipping off the log. She saw the boat spinning crazily, upside down, but she didn't see Tiller.

"Tiller!" she shouted, and then again, louder. She didn't recognize her own call, so loud and urgent, like a bellowing bull. "Tillerrrrr!" But there was no answer as she barreled on down the river on her one-log raft.

∞ 53 ∞

The Dunces

"This sure is more than five minutes we've been hiking," Sairy said.

"More like forty-five minutes," Dallas said. "Don't see any sign of a diner. You know what I'm thinking, Sairy? I'm thinking those two boys were pulling our legs. There's no diner out here, and they've probably stolen our backpacks."

Sairy halted, smacking her hand against her forehead. "I am such a dunce sometimes."

"No, you're not," Dallas said. "You just think everybody's good, and that everybody tells the truth."

Sairy put a hand on Dallas's shoulder. "I do think that," she said, "and that's why I'm feeling like such a dunce right now." Sairy untied her yellow scarf and jammed it in her pocket. "Okay, then, us two dunces are going to find a way out of this place."

Overhead the sun was covered with haze. The air felt heavy, steamy, pressing in on them as they continued along the narrow path.

"We better find a town pretty soon," Dallas said. He didn't want to tell Sairy that the awful feeling he'd had about Florida being in trouble was getting stronger. He was certain of it now. She was in trouble, and she was in the river. He knew it as clearly as if he had a crystal ball. "If we find a town, the people in the town will at least know where *they* are, and then we'll know where *we* are. Does that buddy of Tiller's, that Z guy, have a phone?"

"No, but I can leave a message for him at Grace's Diner. He checks in there regularly."

"I think I've seen that guy before," Dallas said. "I think I've seen him with Mr. Trepid."

"No!" Sairy said. "I certainly hope not."

"That Z guy doesn't talk too much, does he?" Dallas said.

"Not too much. He lives by himself, so

he's not used to talking much."

"What happened?" Dallas said. "Did he one time have some brothers or sisters or kids or wife and they all got drowned or killed or something?"

"You're starting to sound like Florida," Sairy said. "I think Z has a brother or two, but they live out west somewhere. I've never met them anyway. And he did have a wife once, but not for long."

Dallas was picturing Z living with his wife, and the two of them strolling through the holler. "What happened to his wife?"

"She didn't much take to living in the holler, I guess. Wanted to see the world. She hated being stuck up there in his little cabin, so one day she up and left."

"Did they have any kids?" Dallas asked.

"No."

"Did he ever see her again?"

"Dallas, you sure ask a lot of questions."

"I was just wondering, that's all. Seems to me if your wife up and left, you'd go after her, wouldn't you?"

"I suppose."

"So why didn't Z go after his wife?"

Sairy picked up a stick lying across the path. "It was a long time ago—ten, maybe fifteen years ago. I think he did go after her, but I don't think he found her."

"That's a shame," Dallas said. He pictured Z sitting all by himself on the porch of his cabin. "Hey! Look—we've been yakking and not paying any attention, and I think we've found a farm. See? Way over there?"

Sairy raised both her arms in the air. "A farm! Civilization! People! A phone! Let's run!"

And the two of them took off, running through the woods, leaping over logs and dodging branches.

Slow Motion

Tiller had been swimming toward Florida when his arms gave out. They were numb and heavy, and he felt crushing pressure against his chest. The water pulled him under, where everything seemed suddenly slow and quiet. Tiller tugged at his jacket, as if that could release the weight against his chest.

A simple, clear image floated through his mind. It was of him, diving into a river after his younger daughter, Rose, had gone under and hadn't surfaced. He found her sitting cross-legged on the bottom, holding her nose. Tiller snagged her arm and pulled her to the surface.

"Aw, Daddy," she'd spluttered. "I almost broke my record!"

Now, underwater, Rose blurred with Florida. He hoped Florida was holding her nose. And then he thought of Sairy, and he wished he'd said he would go with her to search for her rocking bird.

The last thought he had was about how he and Sairy had had to keep one little secret from each other all those years, that understone fund secret, that silly secret. He felt he understood that now. Maybe keeping that secret would be protection, in case something happened to the other person. Then the person remaining would have one thing left to grip on to. Or maybe it was because there might be times, like now, when, if you knew everything about someone else, your heart would be too full and it might overflow.

55

On the Road

As Z drove Sairy and Dallas away from the farm and down the bumpy road, he felt jittery. They had to find Tiller and Florida quick. Sairy and Dallas had made that clear. Z thought it perfectly reasonable that they had sensed that Tiller and Florida were in trouble. The mind worked in strange ways, he believed.

Z kept stealing glances at Dallas. *He doesn't look anything like me,* Z thought. *Fortunate for him. I'm an ugly son-of-a-gun.*

"What do you think, Z?" Sairy said. "How are we going to gauge where they might be on that river?"

"Not sure," Z said. "We're going to go with

our gut feelings." He sped over the bumpy road and careened out onto the highway. *I should have shaved,* he thought. *I should have changed clothes. That kid must think I'm a bum.*

"There's something I ought to tell you," Z said. "About that Trepid fellow—"

"He stole the understone funds?" Dallas blurted. "He's been down in the holler poking around, and—"

"Dallas! What on earth would put that in your head?" Sairy said.

"Well, he ain't far off," Z said. "He's a mighty smart cookie. He must have some of that extra-sensory whatever, you know, reading people's minds and such."

"Huh?" Sairy said. "What's going on?"

So Z filled them in on how Mr. Trepid had asked him to check out the holler and find any "special stones" and make a map.

"So you think he's looking for our understone funds?" Sairy asked.

"Yep."

"How on earth would he have heard about our understone funds? I can't for the life of me imagine who could've told him. I know you wouldn't tell him, Z."

"You got that right," Z said.

Dallas opened his mouth, closed it, opened it again.

"I got a little confession, though," Z said. "I took your funds. For safekeeping."

"How'd you find them?" Dallas said.

"Got a nose for buried things, I guess," Z said. "Don't worry, Sairy. It's all safe."

"I'm not worried," she said. "Not about that—"

"Got the two metal boxes," Z said, "and the loose money in those other two holes—"

"What other two holes?" Sairy asked.

"Probably mine and Florida's," Dallas said.

Sairy touched Dallas's hand. "You mean you two have your own understone funds? Just like me and Tiller?" A little sound, like a stifled sob, came from her mouth. "That's so . . . so . . . sweet," she said.

Dallas felt terrible. He wished he could disappear into the seat. Not only was he feeling guilty about having told Mr. Trepid about the understone funds, but he feared they wouldn't find Florida and Tiller, or that if they found them, they might be dead. Instantly, his mind moved elsewhere, to the holler, to the cabin, to the loft, to the bed with its soft quilts.

"So is that Trepid fellow still going to be nosing around the holler?" Sairy asked.

"Good question," Z said.

Dallas studied Sairy. He knew she was as worried as he was about Tiller and Florida, because of the way she was wringing that yellow scarf in her hands and staring intently at the road ahead, as if staring would get them there faster. Dallas turned to look at Z, who maneuvered his truck around the curves as if he were an expert race car driver.

"You know that Kangadoon place?" Z said. "I've been doing some asking around, and found a guy who's been there."

It was hard for Dallas to keep his mind on the conversation. Why was Z chattering away about Kangadoon? Why wasn't he coming up with a plan to find Tiller and Florida?

"So what'd that guy say about Kanga-doon?" Sairy asked.

Dallas wanted to scream. *Shut up about Kangadoon!*

Z slapped at the dashboard. "He got eaten nearly alive by mosquitoes! Came home with malaria."

"Malaria?" Sairy said.

"Yep." Z swerved off the main road and down a narrower one. "This here road goes to the Mackalack River," he said. "That's where my gut is telling me to go. What're your guts telling you?"

Dallas pressed his hand against his stomach and closed his eyes. "Mackalack," he said. "Sounds right to me."

56

On the River

With the help of her one-log raft, Florida had made her way to the bank and crawled up its muddy side. She lay there for a minute, trying to catch her breath, and then she sat up and scanned the water. She was feeling a little mad at Tiller, that he hadn't rescued her.

Florida spotted the boat, stuck in the mud upstream, on the same side of the river. She saw one life jacket bobbing against the opposite bank.

"Till-errr!" she shouted. She saw a flash of color upstream, near a boulder. Tiller's jacket? Then she saw his head bob up and go back down.

She raced upstream and tugged at the boat,

flipping it over. No paddles. She saw Tiller's jacket and head bob up again and go down. She hurried to untie the tent ropes from the struts, and then tied one end to a tree on the bank. Holding the other end in her hand, she waded back into the water.

"Till-errrr!" she shouted. "I'm coming! I'm coming through this putrid stupid river. I'm probably going to die doing it, but I'm coming. I hope you appreciate this."

The water pushed at her, whirling and swirling around her knees and then her waist and chest. Knocked and dragged by the current, Florida held tight to the rope, her eyes fixed on flashes of Tiller's jacket, which ballooned up out of the river and skittered in the air before settling back down again.

"Listen, river," she said, as she inched along the river bottom, "I'll make you a deal. You let up on me and I'll . . . I'll . . ." but she couldn't think of what bargain she could make with the river. "Sweet river," she tried, "beautiful river—" but the water surged at her, knocking her under. She pulled herself upright with the rope.

"Cruddy, scummy, pea-brained river."

Tiller's jacket billowed up again, and she lunged, snagging the jacket and pulling it toward her. She grabbed Tiller's arm, wrapped the rope around it, and fished under the water for his head.

When she saw his face, she wanted to bust out crying. *Oh man, Tiller, you are not looking so good. You are looking purely dead.*

She dragged him to the bank and rolled him on his stomach and mashed on his back. She wished she'd paid more attention in health class, when that nurse had come in with a rubber dummy and showed how to do that artificial perspiration stuff.

A splurt of water gushed from Tiller's mouth. Florida rolled him onto his side and probed her finger in his mouth to see if anything was stuck in there. All the while, she was shouting at him. "Tiller! Tiller! You hear me? You breathing? I don't want to have to do that breathing stuff. I don't know how. I don't remember."

She pinched Tiller's nose and thought of

Dallas trying to breathe air into Joey. As she was about to breathe into Tiller's mouth, his eyes opened.

"I sure hope that means you're alive!" she said. "I hope you're not going to putrid die on me."

Tiller raised one hand and placed it against his chest, patting it. "My heart's feeling soggy," he said. "Get help." His eyes closed again.

"Well, where am I supposed to get help?" she said. "Wake up. Don't you putrid die." She scanned the banks, and then she shouted the only thing she could think of to shout: "Dallas! Dal-las!"

Z and Sairy and Dallas, who were downstream searching the banks, heard her. When Florida saw them running toward her, she felt as if she would break apart into a zillion pieces, and all those pieces would scatter into the air and disappear into the clouds.

57

The Soggy Heart

Florida was in the hospital waiting room, wrapped in a blanket. Beside her were Dallas and Z.

"I'm just glad you were there, Florida," Sairy had said, before she hurried down the hall with the doctor. "I'm so eternally grateful for that. But I'm also sorry you were there, sorry you had to be so scared."

Florida tucked her chin inside the blanket to try to stop its quivering.

"How come we have to wait so long?" Dallas asked. "When are they going to tell us if Tiller will make it?"

Z sat up straighter. *The boy is asking me a*

question. The boy is relying on me. "I'll go ask at the desk," Z said, trying to sound as if he knew what he was doing.

Dallas inched closer to Florida. "It'll be okay, I know it. Don't be worrying, Florida. Nothing can happen to Tiller."

Florida's chin dipped lower into the blanket. She hadn't known she could worry so much about someone other than Dallas. She wanted to run down the hall and bang on all the doors until she found Tiller, and then she wanted to make him better and hear him talk again in his grumpy way and see his grin when he made a joke and watch him flip pancakes and talk about secret recipes.

Z returned, awkwardly shuffling his feet, his hands hanging helplessly by his sides. "They don't know much yet," he said. Z stuffed his hands in his pockets and then pulled them out again. "Hospitals make me a little crazy. I'm gonna go find us some doughnuts." And with that, he hurried from the room.

"Kind of a strange guy, that Z," Dallas said.

Florida, spotting Sairy coming toward

them, leaped up and raced toward her. She buried her head against Sairy, wrapping her arms tightly around her. "Maggoty river," she said.

"It's okay," Sairy said, stroking Florida's hair. "I think our Tiller's going to make it."

58

Preparations

Z and Dallas and Florida were in the kitchen with Sairy. Bowls and measuring cups and ingredients covered the counters; flour and sugar dusted their clothes.

"Sairy, you should see the gop we got," Florida said. "Tell her, Dallas. Tell her about all our gunk."

"We've got mousetraps and lizards and worms and thumbtacks and nettles and—"

Florida jumped in. "—and poison ivy and mashed blackberries and a dead mouse. Found the dead putrid mouse by the barn."

"Soon as we do our digging," Sairy said, "I'll go on back to the hospital. Tiller will be sorry he missed this, though."

"His heart attack is over, though, right?" Florida said. "It was only a little one, right?"

"He'll be fine," Sairy said. "He's already grumbling, so I know he'll be just fine. We might be able to bring him home today."

Z sniffed the air. "What're you cooking?"

"Be-nice-to-orphans brownies," Sairy said. "Might not work, but what the heck. Worth a try."

Outside, they dug beneath the marked stones and inserted the brownies in one hole, and the mousetraps and lizards and worms and thumbtacks and nettles and poison ivy and mashed blackberries and dead mouse in the other holes.

"Now, for the final one," Z said. "Picked these up at Vinnie's Variety, just like Dallas suggested." He held a bag out to show them.

The previous night, after Z had left Ruby Holler, he drove into Boxton. In the alley, he saw Mr. Trepid scooting back and forth, peering out into the black night.

Z passed him a folded piece of paper. "Took longer than I expected," Z said. "Lot of territory up there. Lot of stones."

Mr. Trepid hurriedly unfolded the paper and aimed a flashlight at it. "Ah," he said, and "So," and "My, my." He studied the paper. "Still seems like a lot of sites—"

"Like I said, there's a lot of stones up there. I tried to narrow it down, like you said." Z leaned against the shack and gazed out into the dark night. "So, what's next?"

Mr. Trepid flicked off the flashlight. "I'll take care of it from here on. Your work is done."

"What about the additional salary?" Z asked.

"Like I said, if this produces results, you'll get your bonus."

"And when are you likely to know if there's any *results*?"

"When did you say they're coming back?" Trepid asked.

"About a week, as far as I can gather," Z lied.

"I'd better get busy then," Trepid said. "I should know the results before they get back."

"If you're going up there, I'd say Sunday would be best, just to be on the safe side."

"Fine, fine," Trepid said, motioning Z away. "Off with you then. I've got things to do. Things to do!"

Later, alone in the shack, Mr. Trepid studied the map. *A treasure map.* He could hardly contain himself. Leaning against the table was a shovel, and on the table was a trowel and a sturdy empty sack. Mr. Trepid rubbed his hands together. *A treasure map for Ruby Holler.*

59

Investments

Mrs. Trepid was furious. "What do you mean, you'll be away all day?" she asked her husband. "What am I supposed to do with all those kids once they get back from Sunday School? You know Morgan's off this morning. I can't manage all these rowdy kids by myself."

Mr. Trepid rummaged in the closet until he found his old boots. "I told you, this is important," he said. "It concerns the . . . the *investments*."

"Where would you be going dressed like that, in that old bowling shirt and those dirty boots? That doesn't look like investment-checking clothing to me."

Mr. Trepid scurried past her to a chair, where he sat and stuffed his feet into the boots.

"Do that outside," Mrs. Trepid said. "You're getting dried-up old mud on the carpet. Just like the kids."

He ignored her, lacing his boots and scooting over to the closet again.

"You didn't answer me," Mrs. Trepid said. "How am I supposed to manage all these kids on my own, and where are you going dressed like that?"

He turned and smiled sweetly at her. "I am sure you can manage one day on your own, and as for where I'm going, you needn't worry your pretty little head about that," he said.

Mrs. Trepid hated whenever he referred to her *pretty little head*. It made her feel like a stupid little doll thing. "My pretty little head," she said icily, "would just like to know where you are going. My pretty little head does not think that is too much to ask her husband."

There was one thing about his wife that Mr. Trepid particularly disliked. When she wanted to know something, she would hammer him to death with questions until he answered her.

"I am checking on some land investments," he said. "So I need to go look at the land. The land is out in the country. If these investments come through, we will not have to clean up after these kids anymore. We will go to an island in the deep blue sea. There! Is your pretty little head satisfied?"

Mrs. Trepid didn't answer him. She was looking at herself in the mirror, remembering the pale blue silk dress with the pink flowers and the gold necklace with rubies and opals.

60

Hospital Talk

Sairy was seated in a chair beside Tiller's hospital bed.

"I want to get out of here," Tiller grumbled. "Feel fine. Don't like being cooped up like this. I want my creaky swing and lopsided porch. Don't want anybody poking around in here"—he tapped at his chest—"cutting me open and messing around with things."

"You sure are grumpy," Sairy said. "The doctor said you don't need that bypass operation after all. With a little rest and watching your diet, you'll feel like a new man in no time."

"Bypass! Makes me sound like a road. And

I don't want to be a new man. I want to be the old me."

"The old, crotchety boot I know so well?" Sairy asked.

"The *handsome* old, crotchety boot."

They'd been talking most of the afternoon, full up to the top of their heads with things to say, and what they had to say wasn't about each other or about their trips or even about heart attacks or bypass operations. It was about the Hoppers and Cranbeps and Burgertons and Dreeps and Trepids and the Boxton Creek Home.

"We can't let Dallas and Florida go back to that place," Sairy said.

"I know it," Tiller said.

"Those Trepid people shouldn't be running a home for kids."

"I know it."

"Tiller? I love those two kids. I love them to pieces, like they're our own kids."

"I know it."

"Z said there are about a dozen kids in that Home," Sairy said. "Poor things. It's a crime.

You think they're all feeling as jittery as Dallas and Florida were when they first came here? Remember? How they thought we were going to make them sleep in a hog pen?"

"Or was it a snake pit?"

"I just can't hardly bear to part with those two," Sairy said.

"I know it."

"And Tiller? I love the holler, too. I just want you to know that."

"I know it."

"And Tiller? Without you, I'm just a sock without a boot."

"I know it." He gazed at Sairy. "Do you want me to say all those nice things back to you?"

"No," she said, tapping his chest. "I know it all."

"Good."

"So," Sairy said, "You got any ideas? Can you think of any way to keep Dallas and Florida in the holler?"

"I'll sleep on it," he said. "I'll sleep on it real good." Tiller leaned back, closed his eyes, and quickly opened them again. "Hey," he said. "I just remembered something. When Z was in here, he said he had something he wanted to discuss with me after I get home. What do you think that's about?"

Sairy yawned. "Oh, probably nothing important. You know what he asked me? If I remembered what year his wife left! I told him I hadn't the foggiest recollection. Now take a nap while we wait for the doctor to set you free. You need to rest up. Buddy and Lucy are arriving on Monday."

"Aw, they don't need to come all the way down here," Tiller said. "That makes me nervous, kids gathering around like I'm going to kick the bucket."

"And we've got that little Trepid adventure tomorrow, don't forget."

"Trepid? That putrid—" Tiller pushed the covers aside and swung his feet over the side of the bed. "No time for napping. Where are my clothes? Where's that doctor? Get me out of here."

Mr. Trepid's Adventure

O n Sunday, Mr. Trepid turned off the main highway and drove down a narrower side road and then onto a bumpy dirt road which led into Ruby Holler. He didn't see how anyone could live out here. Bumpy roads and no signs, no stores, no gas stations. What did a person do if he ran out of gas? What if he got hungry?

As his car clunked and bumped along, Mr. Trepid thought about the red Cadillac convertible. He imagined himself driving along on a day such as this, with the top down, his arm along the door, the wind breezing by. He glanced over at where his wife would be sitting, her head leaning back against the seat, the

wind blowing her hair. She wouldn't be pep-
pering him with questions. No, she'd be smiling to herself, happy to be riding along in a red
Cadillac convertible with her husband.

That old couple who lived up in the holler,
what did they need so much money for? *If
they were stupid enough to bury it in a hole*, he
thought, *then they're practically begging for someone to find it and take it*. If a person like himself
was just out digging on a hillside and happened to find something, it was his, right?
Finders keepers.

When he reached the end of the dirt road,
Mr. Trepid got out of the car and retrieved his
shovel, trowel, and sack from the trunk. He patted his shirt pocket to be sure the map was still
there and set off down the path.

When he found the cabin, he studied the
map, paced twenty feet away from the cabin,
and spotted the first pile of stones. Quickly, he
moved the rocks aside and plunged the trowel
into the dirt.

In the barn loft, Dallas aimed his binoculars
at Mr. Trepid, Florida aimed a camera, and Sairy

and Tiller kneeled behind them. Z was perched in a tree near the bear bush.

Two hours later, Mr. Trepid was spitting mad. Dotted across the hillside were the remains of his digging efforts: stones and dirt cast aside in sloppy heaps. It looked as if a crowd of moles had engaged in a burrowing frenzy.

He had not yet found the piles of money he was looking for, but he had unearthed some strange things. One was a packet of brownies. He'd tentatively tasted one. *Not bad,* he thought, *but why are they burying food? Are they crazy?* In one hole, he'd found only a tangle of leaves and berries, and in another, a mousetrap, which snapped on his thumb. He'd plunged his hand into a pile of stinging nettles in one hole, and into a clump of mashed blackberries wrapped deceptively in a leather pouch in another hole. He was nursing a dozen tiny thumbtack-pricks and a peculiar rash creeping up his arm.

When Mr. Trepid had lifted one of the more promising-looking stones, three lizards raced across his boots, and one darted up his pant leg. Without thinking, he smashed the shovel against his leg. The lizard fell out, stunned, but now his leg was sore and bruised. That was pretty much the last straw for Mr. Trepid.

Those conniving people, he thought. *They have purposely put this stuff here to mislead anyone who might come looking.* He studied the map. He'd investigated all but one of the holes and wondered if he should just give up and go home. Who knew what might be under that last pile of stones. Maybe a poisonous snake? Maybe something worse?

Mr. Trepid made his way to the last stone marked on the map, kicking dirt clogs ahead of him, and smashing his shovel into tree trunks. When he reached the stone, he knelt down. This one had black swirly lines on it. *Maybe a code?* He tapped at the stone with his shovel, debating whether to move the stone and dig underneath. *Oh well,* he thought, *it's the last one. Might as well try. I have got to find that money. I can't go home empty-handed.*

The shovel snagged what appeared to be a

length of cord. He snatched at it, releasing a pouch from the dirt. *Here we go again. Probably some stupid food.* Nudging the sack with the toe of his boot, he felt something hard inside. He nudged again. Many hard little things. Marbles? Pebbles?

He probed at the opening of the pouch with a stick, loosening it. Carefully, he took hold of the bottom of the pouch and tipped its contents out onto the ground.

Yes! he thought. *Payday!* He could hardly believe his eyes.

ᢏᢌ 62 ᢏᢌ

Jewels

Mr. and Mrs. Trepid sat on the edge of their bed, staring at the contents of the pouch, which Mr. Trepid had emptied on the bedspread.

"Look at that," Mr. Trepid said, scratching fiercely at the rash spreading up his arms. "Look at all those jewels!"

Mrs. Trepid reached out tentatively, touching one of the red stones. "Rubies?" she said.

Mr. Trepid gathered a handful of stones and let them fall back on the bedspread, where they scattered like colorful raindrops. "Rubies and emeralds and diamonds!"

"But are you sure?" she said.

Mr. Trepid laughed, dizzy with excitement. "What else could they be?"

"But I thought you said . . . wasn't it a land investment you mentioned?"

"Look what I found in the land," he said. "We're rich. We're bazillionaires!" He scratched at his neck. "This stupid rash."

Mrs. Trepid felt faint. She picked up one of the rubies, turning it around in her hand. "It's so smooth," she said.

A knock at their door was followed by Morgan's saying, "Ma'am? It's me, Chief Gopher."

"Quick," Mr. Trepid said, pulling the covers over the jewels. "Hide these."

"Ma'am?" Morgan called. "The baby is dressed. What do you want me to do with her?"

Mrs. Trepid went to the door and opened it a crack. "Just take care of her, Morgan. We have some important business to do." She closed the door and said to her husband, "Well? What now? How do you turn those jewels into money?"

Mr. Trepid had been thinking about that. He'd go to the jeweler's, to the place where he'd looked at that nine-thousand-dollar watch. He'd take a few of the gems and see if the jeweler could give him an estimate of their worth. *Won't he be surprised?* Mr. Trepid thought. *Wait until he sees what we have!*

To his wife, Mr. Trepid said, "I'll be taking these in for appraisal."

"Do you think . . . might I . . . may I keep one of those?" she asked.

Mr. Trepid beamed. "But of course," he said generously. He selected a ruby and placed it in her hand. "For you: a ruby." He gathered up two more stones and dropped them one by one into her open palm. "And an emerald and a diamond."

The three gems sparkled in her hand. *A ruby. An emerald. A diamond.*

"Where'd those brownies come from?" she asked.

"Oh. Stopped at a bake sale on the way home," he lied. "They're not bad. Try one."

As Mrs. Trepid nibbled at a brownie, she heard shouting and the sounds of many feet tramping down the hallway. "And that island you mentioned?" she said to Mr. Trepid. "How soon do you think—?"

"As soon as possible," Mr. Trepid said. "I can smell the sea breeze already." He rubbed furiously at his cheek. "Got any lotion? I must've picked up something out there in the country. It's driving me crazy."

Mission-Accomplished Cake

Tiller, Sairy, Dallas, Florida, and Z were in the cabin kitchen, all tossing ingredients into a big red bowl.

"This is our mission-accomplished cake," Sairy said.

"Needs lots of good stuff in it," Tiller said. "You see anything you want to add, dump it in."

Florida added chocolate syrup. "Boy, that Mr. Trepid was hopping mad when those lizards got him."

Dallas drizzled some honey into the bowl. "And what about when that mousetrap snapped? Man, I could hear him swearing all the way up in the barn."

"Can't wait to get these pictures developed," Z said. "Especially the one of him with the *jewels*."

"Jewels!" Sairy said. "What a foolish man."

"How much did those stones cost?" Tiller asked.

"Got the whole bag for a dollar ninety-nine." Z dropped a handful of pecans into the bowl.

"I do feel a tiny bit bad for Mr. Trepid," Sairy said.

"Don't you go feeling sorry for him," Florida said. "He'd have stolen all your money if he'd had the chance."

"Putrid pincher," Tiller said, adding more chocolate syrup to the bowl.

Z tossed a handful of chopped cherries into the mix. "So what about your trips, your real trips? Guess you're not going on those, right?"

"Tiller and I were talking about that earlier," Sairy said. "Seems we won't be going off on those trips after all. Seems we'll stay right here in the holler." She turned to Florida and Dallas. "I hope you kids aren't going to be too disappointed about that."

Dallas spotted a jar of peanuts, opened it, and dumped them in the bowl. He didn't know what to think. Part of him was relieved, and part of him wanted to bawl his head off.

"Guess I'd better head out to pick up Buddy and Lucy at the airport," Z said. "Be good to have your own kids home, won't it?"

Sairy and Tiller nodded. "It will," they said.

Florida emptied the jar of chocolate syrup into the bowl. She reached across the counter for a bag of cookies, smashed the whole bag with the empty jar, and then emptied the smashed cookies into the bowl.

Sairy cupped Florida's chin in her hands. "Honey," Sairy said, "don't you ever let anyone treat you bad ever again, you hear?"

Sure, Florida thought. *Easy for you to say when you're about to get rid of us.* She pounded the dough with a wooden spoon.

Appraisals

Once again, Mr. Trepid had parked his battered old car several blocks from the Cadillac showroom. He'd worn his best suit, unaware that a piece of bubble gum was stuck to the back of his jacket and that cornflake crumbs clung to his pant legs.

The salesman who had waited on him before met him just inside the door. "Mr. Trepid, correct?" He shook Mr. Trepid's hand, but, noticing the red rash on Mr. Trepid's hand and wrist, the salesman cut short the handshake. "The red Cadillac convertible—is that the one you're still interested in?" The salesman noticed the tiny blisters on Mr. Trepid's face and neck.

"That's right," Mr. Trepid said, rubbing at the skin beneath his jacket. "I just want to be sure it will be available."

"Oh?" the salesman said. "So you've made your decision?"

"Yes," Mr. Trepid said, pawing at his ear. "I'm off to make some arrangements, and then I'll be back. How soon could I have it?"

"Do you care to discuss the finances?"

"No, no. Not now. It'll be fine, I'm sure. I suppose I ought to take it for a test drive. Is that possible?"

"Absolutely," the salesman said. He didn't think he should mention the gum on Mr. Trepid's jacket or the crumbs on his pants. The salesman figured that if a man wanted to buy a new Cadillac, he could have food all over himself if he wanted.

Mr. Trepid parked the Cadillac directly in front of the First Avenue Jewelry store. The *ding* of the door's bell brought the salesman from the back of the store.

"Ah," he said, "Mr. Trepid, I believe?" As Mr. Trepid approached, the salesman noticed

the angry rash creeping up Mr. Trepid's neck
and across his face, and the salesman took a step
backward. He hoped that whatever Mr. Trepid
had wasn't contagious.

"That watch I was looking at, you remember which one?" Mr. Trepid said.

"Yes sir, I do," the salesman said. "Would the
gentleman like to see it again?"

"No, just checking. I wonder if you also do
appraisals?"

"Appraisals? Of jewelry?"

"Yes, or gems? Precious jewels?" Mr. Trepid
retrieved the pouch from his jacket pocket and
laid it carefully on the counter. "I have here
some gems that I'd like appraised."

The man eyed the pouch. "I would be happy
to do appraisals for you. What sort of gems?"

Mr. Trepid raked at his neck. *This blasted rash.*
"Rubies," he said, "and emeralds and diamonds."

"Rubies and emeralds and diamonds? May
I?" The salesman extended his hand.

Mr. Trepid smiled as he carefully undid the
pouch and poured the gems into the salesman's
hand.

The salesman stared at the stones and cleared his throat. "Perhaps you would like to leave them with me," he said. "I will need to . . . to consult my manager."

"Fine, fine, whatever," Mr. Trepid said. "When do you think you can give me a firm appraisal?"

The salesman dumped the stones back into the pouch. "Oh, I'd say by tomorrow, no problem."

"And my gems are safe here with you?" Mr. Trepid said.

The salesman chewed on his lip. "Oh yes, they're perfectly safe with me."

"Fine, fine, very good then," Mr. Trepid said.

As Mr. Trepid drove away, the salesman called to someone in the back room. "Hey, get in here. Wait'll you see what this joker wants appraised. A bunch of worthless dime-store stones!"

65

Conversations in the Night

It was a cool night in the holler, with a lazy breeze blowing through, whisking branches against the loft window. Dallas whispered to Florida. "Listen. Hear Tiller snoring? And can you hear Sairy and her kids down there? They're still talking."

"Don't they know we can hear them?" Florida said. She was hidden under her quilt, with only her head poking out, staring at Buddy's and Lucy's suitcases sitting on the two empty beds.

"Tiller and Sairy seem pretty happy to see their kids, don't they?" Dallas said.

"Don't talk about it. They're probably sorry we're taking up space here. Did you hear what

Buddy said when he saw us? He said, 'Who are those two kids?'—like we were a couple of dogs."

"He didn't mean it like that," Dallas said.

Florida had also heard Lucy ask her parents what on earth those two kids were doing here, and what on earth had Tiller and Sairy been thinking, anyway, taking on a couple of stray kids that they didn't know anything about. Florida could hear Lucy's voice now, below, rising as if she were annoyed.

"You can't possibly keep them here now," Lucy said. "What with Dad recuperating and—"

"Shh," Sairy said. "Lower your voice, please."

"But Mom—" Lucy said.

"Let's go outside," Sairy said.

Florida heard the screen door close and then turned to Dallas. "We're just in the way," she said. "I thought Tiller and Sairy were different from all the rest of those trouble grown-ups, but they're not."

"Stop it," Dallas said. "They *are* different. Don't you go talking bad about them."

"I can say whatever I want," she said. She thought about Tiller lying in his bed downstairs.

What was Tiller dreaming? What if his heart started hurting again?

Dallas was out of bed, rummaging around.

"What're you doing?" Florida said. "What're you stuffing in that sack?"

"I'm packing."

"Don't do that," Florida said.

"Why not? Maybe you're right. Maybe our time is up here. They don't need us, and we're in the way, aren't we?" Dallas put a change of clothes in the sack and then pulled them out again. "What's ours and what's theirs? Is this shirt mine?"

"Of course it's yours, Dallas. Who else's would it be?"

"I mean did they buy it, or did I have it already when we came here?"

"Let me see it," Florida said.

Dallas tossed the shirt at her.

"You don't have to be so rough," she said, examining the shirt. "It's a nice one. Definitely not one you had when we came here." She tossed it back to Dallas, who threw it on the floor.

Reluctantly, Florida eased out from under the quilt. "I guess I've got to pack, too," she said.

"I guess you do," Dallas said, "unless you're not coming with me."

"What're you talking about? You wouldn't go without me, would you?"

Dallas sat back down on his bed. "No, I wouldn't do that. Not if you wanted to come. But maybe you don't want to come. Maybe that night freight train doesn't sound so good to you anymore."

"It sounds good. It sounds just fine. I'm just tired is all. I thought we'd be resting up a few days," Florida said. She was surprised at how much she didn't want to leave.

"No point in resting up," Dallas said. "Might as well get moving."

"Are you talking about *tonight*?" Florida asked. "You mean like this night here, right now?"

"That's what I mean," Dallas said. "After Lucy and Buddy are asleep."

"But what about saying good-bye? We're not even going to say good-bye?"

It was nearly midnight when Lucy and Buddy crept up to the loft and Sairy crawled into bed beside Tiller. She studied his face and listened to his even breathing. She sat leaning against the headboard, knowing she would have trouble sleeping.

She'd been surprised when Lucy and Buddy suggested that Dallas and Florida should be sent back to the Home right away. Could this be her own Lucy, her own Buddy—so cold, so unfeeling? Then Sairy told Buddy and Lucy about the Trepids, and about the Hoppers and the Cranbeps and Burgertons and Dreeps. She told them about Florida and Tiller fixing up the old boat, and about Dallas helping her plan her trip and get supplies, and about how the kids had run through the holler and climbed its trees.

"Oh, Mom," Lucy had said when she finished. "They must love the holler, just like we all did. I dream of it all the time. And to be back here now, oh . . ."

Buddy was sitting on the porch swing, taking in the view. "What a place this is. What a place!" He took ahold of Sairy's hand. "But are you sure you can manage two kids right now? Are you sure you can handle something else to worry about?"

"Worry about?" Sairy had said. "Those two *keep* us from worrying. They're a comfort."

But now, as she lay in bed, she wondered if it was selfish of her to want Dallas and Florida to stay. What was the best thing for them? Certainly it was not going back to the Home. She was sure of that. And those kids loved the holler. They loved being able to run and shout. They loved the stream and the trees and the birds.

She wanted to wake Tiller, so that he could reassure her. In the hospital, he'd said one of the first things he was going to do when he'd rested up was to teach Dallas how to chop wood and light the lanterns. And he'd go fishing with Florida and teach her how to swim.

She heard Buddy and Lucy climb into their beds above, and then it was quiet, with only the wind brushing the branches against the house.

"Good night, Tiller," she whispered. "Good night, my handsome old boot."

Florida heard Dallas slip out of bed. What she really wanted to do was stay under her quilt and drift off to sleep and wake to the smell of bacon and eggs and waffles and syrup and honey and blueberries and everything sweet and warm that you could possibly think of to eat.

"It's time," Dallas whispered.

"What's that? A note?"

"Yeah. I'll leave it on the bureau. I'm leaving that carving, too."

"That leafy-tree one? Okay, I'll leave mine, too."

"What is it?"

"A curly-headed bat." She knew that bats didn't really have curly heads, but that's how this one came out. And bats were good. Tiller had said so. She watched Dallas stuff his old socks into his sack. "Hey, Dallas, whatever happened to your backpack? And your sleeping bag?"

"Lost them," he said, thinking about the two boys who had offered to "watch" his and Sairy's gear. Maybe the gear was still there. Maybe he could find his way back.

"You ready?" Florida asked, interrupting his thoughts.

"What? Oh yeah. Okay. Ready."

They slipped down the ladder and out the door. "Okay," Dallas said, trying to sound more cheerful than he felt. "Let's catch that night train and ride on out of town!"

They had just stepped off the porch when Florida said, "Hey, wait. What about our money?"

"Shoot. Z's got it, remember? Guess we could try and find his place and ask him for our money."

"Forget it," Florida said. "We've got no dang idea where his place is. Money is trouble, Dallas. I don't want it."

Dallas thought about all the food their money could buy, and his stomach rumbled in response. Maybe they should wait another day and get their money from Z.

But they were outside, and they were on their way, and their feet kept moving forward.

Across the holler, Z was in his own cabin, holding a lantern in the middle of the main room. *What a pit. Maybe I oughta start cleaning. Maybe I oughta get some groceries. Maybe I oughta . . .* But he didn't do anything except flop down on his bed and go to sleep.

66

Dreams

When there is a full moon in Ruby Holler, as there was on the night that Dallas and Florida left the cabin, the purest silver light makes everything above and below look soft and rich, like velvet. The birds sit quietly in the trees, and all the other creatures seem to move more gently, as if their feet are padded with cotton.

"Good smell here," Florida said, as they picked their way along beside the barn. "Good old barn, too."

Dallas leaned forward to smell the wood siding. "Let's follow the creek a ways," he said.

They wound their way down the hill and

moved slowly along the bank, picking their way over stones and around bushes until Florida said, "Wait. Stop."

"What's the matter?"

"I don't want to leave," Florida said. "I like it here. Nobody ever treated us this good before, and nobody's probably ever going to treat us this good again."

"But like you said, maybe we're in the way now. We don't have any choice, do we?" Dallas said.

"Who's going to chop the wood while Tiller's getting his strength back?" Florida said. "And who's going to haul the water?"

Dallas saw himself, Pioneer Boy, chopping wood and hauling water. He saw himself stalking through the woods—

"And," Florida said, "who's going to help Sairy with all those getting-over-heart-attack things she's going to have to make? Answer me that."

Dallas stood there, thinking. "I believe I'm getting a little idea," he said. "Are you getting an idea?"

"Yep," she said.

Dallas glanced around. "Whoa!" He moved toward a tree near the bank, a tall one, with long leafy branches dipping toward the ground. "In here," he said, dipping under the branches.

"It's like a fort or something," Florida said.

"I've had a dream about this place," Dallas said. "Honest, it was this exact place, this leafy tree with the branches hanging down, and the creek nearby. What an odd thing, that it's a real place."

"Dallas? Let's camp here, okay?"

"You mean camp here and—"

"—and see what happens." Florida spread out her sleeping bag and crawled inside. "You going to be okay without a sleeping bag, Dallas?"

"Yeah," he said. "I've got this sack for a pillow, and maybe the crawly things will leave me alone for one night."

"Dallas? Are you hoping what I'm hoping?"

"Maybe," he said. "Let's not say it out loud, though."

And so they slept, and as they slept, they dreamed again of talking birds. Florida was paddling down the river on a raft when a meteor crossed the sky, filling it with golden light, and out of the golden light came a golden bird, which swept down to Florida's raft. It said, "You're my baby," and Florida put out her hand to the bird and said, "Okay."

In Dallas's dream, he crawled out from beneath the leafy tree and stood by the edge of the clear stream. Soon a silver bird fluttered down from the sky and sat on his shoulder. "There is a place where you can go, where everything is—"

"Is what?" Dallas said.

"—where everything is magic," the bird said.

Dallas touched the silver feathers. "And that place is . . . ?"

But the bird merely tucked its head in its wing and fell asleep.

In the morning, Dallas heard the birds calling and knew it was first light, but he didn't open his eyes. He held very still, afraid to breathe.

Florida, too, heard the birds. *Oh please,* she prayed, *please.* She scrambled out of her sleeping bag and breathed deeply.

"Dallas, wake up!" she called.

Dallas lifted his head and glanced at Florida.

"Dallas, take a whiff. What's that you smell?"

He inhaled. It was the best smell in the world.

Bacon. Welcome-home bacon.